STAR WARS®
GALAXY of FEAR

PLANET PLAGUE

Slime time on Planet Plague . . .

Tash's heart was pounding. The hallway was dim, lit only by small glowpanels placed far apart. She wondered how far she was inside the ziggurat. She guessed that she must be close to the bottom.

Tash heard a soft, squishing sound echo faintly behind her. She quickly glanced over her shoulder.

No one was there.

She took a few more steps, and heard the *squish* again.

She looked back. The hallway was still empty.

Then Tash looked up.

Over her head hung several oozing blobs, ready to drop.

Look for a preview of Star Wars: Galaxy of Fear #4, *The Nightmare Machine,* in the back of this book!

STAR WARS®
GALAXY of FEAR

BOOK 3
PLANET PLAGUE

JOHN WHITMAN

BANTAM BOOKS
NEW YORK · TORONTO · LONDON · SYDNEY · AUCKLAND

*To my editors, Karen Meyers and Sue Rostoni, plagued by
tardy writers!*

RL 6.0, 008–012

PLANET PLAGUE

A Bantam Skylark Book / April 1997

Skylark Books is a registered trademark of Bantam Books, a division of Bantam
Doubleday Dell Publishing Group, Inc. Registered in U.S. Patent and Trademark
Office and elsewhere.

ISBN 0-553-48452-4

Published simultaneously in the United States and Canada.

Bantam Books are published by Bantam Books, a division of Bantam Doubleday Dell
Publishing Group, Inc. Its trademark, consisting of the words ''Bantam Books'' and the
portrayal of a rooster, is Registered in U.S. Patent and Trademark Office and in other
countries. Marca Registrada. Bantam Books, 1540 Broadway, New York, New York
10036.

PRINTED IN THE UNITED STATES OF AMERICA
OPM 0 9 8 7 6 5 4 3 2 1

PROLOGUE

With a crackle of energy the image solidified before the scientist's eyes. It was only a hologram, but it was a hologram of the most powerful being the galaxy had ever known.

It was the Emperor himself.

Although the scientist was seated at his control module, at the center of his own network of power, he trembled. He could order the deaths of hundreds if he wished. With his terrible knowledge he could engineer nightmares. But as powerful as the scientist was, the Emperor could snuff him out with little more than a thought.

"What is thy bidding, my lord?" the scientist asked in a trembling voice.

"Your enemies have gained a distinct advantage." Beneath the hood of his plain black robe, the Emperor's ancient face looked wrinkled and frail. But his voice, even though it was beamed from a thousand light-years away, still had evil power. "Failure has become a possibility."

The scientist shuddered. As always the Emperor seemed to learn of events almost before they occurred. He already knew that an intruder named Hoole, along with his droid and two young humans, had ruined the scientist's experiment on D'vouran, the living planet. They had also destroyed his work with the undead on Necropolis.

"M-My lord," the scientist said as confidently as he could manage. "I assure you these incidents have not delayed my work. Hoole is only an overly curious anthropologist, and the two humans are only children. They cannot possibly know our intentions.''

''Do not underestimate the resourcefulness of your enemies.'' The Emperor's eyes darkened. ''That was Grand Moff Tarkin's mistake when he built the Death Star.''

The scientist bowed. The Death Star—a battle station equipped with a planet-destroying laser—was supposed to have been the cornerstone of the Empire's Doctrine of Fear. But the Rebels had managed to destroy it. The scientist would not make the same mistakes as the Death Star's creator. ''My lord, I swear, the next phase of Project Starscream will be delivered on schedule.''

The Emperor gave a slight nod. ''See to it. Personally.'' The ruler's image vanished.

The scientist stood up and regained his composure. He dared not disappoint the Emperor. He would handle the next phase of Project Starscream personally. And if Hoole somehow interfered, the scientist would deal with him personally, too.

The scientist smiled. He knew that Hoole would never suspect that *he* was the enemy.

CHAPTER

Someone was pounding on the door.

"Tash, open up!" It was the voice of her brother, Zak.

"Go away," she warned.

"Come on, it can't be that bad," he argued.

"You think?" Tash yelled through the wall of the room. "Wait until you start getting them." She heard Zak sigh and walk away.

Tash stared at her reflection in the small mirror and groaned.

Tash was thirteen years old. She'd always thought it wouldn't happen to her until she turned fifteen or sixteen.

"There you go," she muttered, "before your time as usual."

She stared at the four red splotches on her face as if glaring would scare them away. But they weren't going anywhere. They sat in the middle of her face, framed by her blonde hair. They were as noticeable as orbital beacons.

To Tash, it was amazing that the intelligent species of the galaxy had learned to travel from one end of the stars to the other, create droids that were as intelligent as humans or any other organic creature, but still no one had come up with a cure for every teenage human's nightmare.

Zits.

She was in the main refresher on board the ship *Shroud*, on which she traveled with her brother, Zak, their uncle Hoole, and his assistant droid DV-9, or Deevee for short. The main 'fresher had the best lighting, and Tash wanted to see just how big her pimples had grown.

Someone pounded on the door again. "Tash!" Zak was back. "Come on, I'm not feeling well. I need the medkit."

"All right!" she said. She opened the door and stared, daring Zak to say something about her face.

But Zak hardly noticed. He went right to the medkit, opened it, and took out two pain relievers, which he quickly swallowed.

"Did Uncle Hoole say you could have those?" she asked.

"Yeah." Zak nodded. "I asked him."

She noticed that her brother's face looked flushed, and

4

he seemed a little sluggish. Zak was a year younger than she was. Normally he was chaotic, unpredictable, and fun-loving. *Not* sluggish.

"Are you getting sick?"

"No way," he responded. "Just a headache from listening to Deevee's lessons. I'm going back to the cockpit. By the way," he added as he went into the hall, "that pimple on your chin is about to go nova!"

Tash grimaced. So much for sympathizing with him. If he was feeling good enough to insult her, he was feeling good enough, period.

Tash went to her cabin and shut the door. The best thing to do about pimples was to wait them out. She had some important work to do in her cabin anyway.

She sat at her small desk, skimming the galactic communications network called the HoloNet on the computer terminal. It was sometimes hard to get a connection in deep space, but Tash had spent hours Net-skimming, and she'd found a way to bounce a computer link off of a deep-space station thirty light-years away, then to planetary antennae in the Corellian system, and finally into the Deep Core Worlds, where the central HoloNet was established.

Tash typed her code name into a message: SEARCHER CALLING FORCEFLOW.

Forceflow was another HoloNet explorer whom Tash had met over a year ago. Forceflow had introduced Tash to the legends of the Jedi Knights, who had been the protectors of the galaxy before the rise of the Empire. She didn't know Forceflow's real name, but she did know that he or she had access to a lot of information.

Tash wasn't looking for information on the Jedi today. She had decided to ask about something more personal.

She was going to ask Forceflow about her uncle.

In the six months that she and Zak had lived with him, Hoole had refused to tell them anything about himself or his work. But over the past few weeks several people had hinted that Hoole was involved in the Empire's shadow world of criminals and assassins. Contacting Forceflow was a long shot, but people in strange places seemed to know their uncle, and Tash's curiosity had gotten the better of her.

After a moment, a line of text appeared on her computer screen.

FORCEFLOW HERE.

HI, she typed. I HAVE A QUESTION FOR YOU. IT'S PRIVATE.

A line appeared in response.

WAIT. I AM CODING OUR TRANSMISSION. There was a pause. When the text continued, it was highlighted in blue, indicating that the HoloNet link had changed. IMPERIAL WATCHDOGS ON MY TAIL. CAN'T TAKE ANY CHANCES.

Tash knew that Forceflow often posted information on the HoloNet that the Empire considered illegal. Even the Jedi lore that she had first discovered was outlawed, but Forceflow had uploaded it anyway. For that reason

Forceflow was often hard to reach, and always very secretive. Tash typed back, IS IT SAFE FOR US TO TALK?

FOR NOW. NO ONE CAN BREAK MY CODES.

GREAT. I WANT TO ASK YOU ABOUT——

But Tash was unable to continue. She nearly fell off her chair as the *Shroud* lurched crazily in space.

CHAPTER 2

For a split second the power was cut off and the lights went out, plunging Tash into darkness. A moment later the lights came back on, but her delicate HoloNet connection had been lost.

"Oh, laser burn," she muttered under her breath. "Zak, you're going to get it for this."

Zak had no interest in piloting, but he was a born tinkerer. Tash would have bet a year's worth of Octavian fruit pudding that he was up in the cockpit right now, taking the console apart.

The ship shook again, and Tash jumped up from her desk, slipping out the automatic door as soon as it opened and hurrying toward the cockpit.

"What's going on up here?" she demanded as she entered the control room. She half-expected to see the navicomputer spread out in pieces on the floor.

Instead she saw Zak slumped over the controls. His head was buried in his folded arms, his face hidden behind his uncontrollable mop of brown hair.

"Zak!" she yelled.

At the sound of her voice, Zak slowly lifted his head and blinked. "Hey, Tash," he said drowsily. "I must have dozed off."

"By the look of things, I would say you fainted," said a low voice behind Tash.

Uncle Hoole had come up behind her without making a sound. Hoole was a member of the Shi'ido species. They were tall, gray humanoids, and stealth was the least of their gifts. The Shi'ido were shape-shifters.

The Shi'ido studied Zak with his dark eyes, and his narrow gray face wrinkled into a frown. "Are you feeling all right?"

Zak sat up straight. His eyelids drooped, and there was a sheen of sweat on his forehead. He still managed a smile. "Me? Sure. I'm prime."

The *Shroud*'s engines let out a groan of distress. Hoole slipped past Tash and examined the readouts quickly. "You laid your head down on the reverse-power coupling controls," Hoole said. "You are flooding too much fuel into the hyperdrive system." Hoole flipped a few switches, and the *Shroud* settled into a smooth flight pattern.

Zak rubbed his eyes and tried to shake his head clear. "Wow, talk about an afternoon nap."

"Try midmorning nap," Tash replied, pointing at the chronometer. Although they were in deep space, the ship's chronometer kept GST, or Galactic Standard Time.

Zak shrugged. "I haven't been this tired since we hiked to the top of the Triplehorn mountains back on Alderaan."

Tash and Uncle Hoole exchanged concerned glances. Zak had been through a lot recently. On their last planetary stop, he had been kidnapped by a wanted criminal named Evazan who was working on some bizarre experiments to bring the dead back to life. Eventually Tash and Hoole had been able to save Zak and to defeat Evazan with the help of the bounty hunter Boba Fett. In fact, they had gotten away in the criminal's own ship, the *Shroud,* in which they now flew.

Despite the terror he'd witnessed, Zak seemed to come out of that frightening experience without any serious harm. Now, however, he looked terrible.

"No way," Zak said, when Tash suggested that what he'd been through might be making him sick. "I'm telling you, I'm as shipshape as an Imperial cruiser." He jumped up and spun unsteadily around on one foot, turning back to face his sister. "I just needed a little sleep, that's all." As if to prove it, Zak wriggled his way past Tash and Hoole and bounded down the corridor to the *Shroud*'s main lounge.

Hoole stared after him. "I'm afraid I have not been around humans long enough to understand your physiology," he said to Tash. "Is this common?"

"I don't know," Tash said. "Back on Alderaan, Mom always seemed to know if we were sick or not."

Tash felt a twinge in her heart when she mentioned her mother. Her parents were dead, thanks to the Empire. They had been on the planet Alderaan when it was blasted into rubble by the Death Star six months ago. Tash tried to swallow a sudden lump in her throat. "I think . . . I think if she were here she'd say Zak was coming down with the flu or something."

"Let us hope it is nothing worse than that," Hoole said. "Zak was in Evazan's hands for some time before we reached him."

"Do you think Evazan might have done something to Zak that we don't know about?"

"I'm not sure," the Shi'ido said, almost to himself. "Let us go see what DV-9 has found in Evazan's computer files."

Evazan was also known as Dr. Death, and his mark was everywhere on the ship he had once owned. The corridors were dark and gloomy. The simple couches in the main lounge were torn and gouged. Beyond the lounge lay a small science laboratory. Hoole and his assistant droid, DV-9, had thrown away specimen jars full of strange matter and cleaned up as much of the lab as they could, but

11

the walls and countertops were still stained with things Tash did not want to think about.

Mechanically, however, the *Shroud* was a first-rate ship, with a high-powered computer system and memory banks filled to capacity with information.

Entering the lab, Tash and Hoole found Deevee at work on the computers, with Zak hovering behind him.

"Zak, you should be in bed," Tash said.

"But look what Deevee's found," he replied.

Deevee had been designed to imitate human functions. He cocked his silver-plated head to one side. "Indeed, this is extremely curious."

"Have you been able to access the files?" Hoole asked.

"In a manner of speaking," Deevee replied. "The files were protected by a security password. My complex logic circuits were a bit rusty from lack of use." The droid glanced disapprovingly at Tash and Zak. Deevee had served as Hoole's research assistant for years. But the day Hoole had volunteered to be guardian of his niece and nephew, Deevee had been assigned as their caretaker, a job he didn't enjoy much. He jumped at any chance to perform the real scientific research he was programmed to do. "But I managed to get *some* real work done." The droid straightened with pride. "It was an extremely complex and difficult password to decipher, but, as you know . . ."

Here it comes, Tash thought.

". . . my computer brain is extremely adaptable to

12

real work such as this, and I was able to decode the password."

"It's something called Project Starscream," Zak said.

"Then we can read the files?" Tash asked.

Deevee looked suddenly deflated. "Well, no. This Evazan must have been quite paranoid. Not only did he install a password, he wrote all the files in code."

Tash peeked around Hoole's shoulder as he studied the computer screen. Lines of gibberish and strings of numbers ran from left to right continuously.

"Can you break this code?" Hoole asked.

"I'm uncertain," the droid confessed.

"What?" Tash couldn't resist joking. "Even with your supercomputer brain?"

Deevee sniffed. "Not even a protocol droid could translate this language. It's far beyond my capacity. I'm afraid I couldn't get any further than the words *Project Starscream*."

"What do you suppose Project Starscream is?" Tash asked.

"Probably none of our concern, I'm sure," Hoole said.

"I bet I could break the code," Zak bragged. "No problem."

"You can barely stand up," Tash said.

"Tash is right," Hoole said. "Zak, I suggest you go to your room and lie down. A real rest may do you good."

To Tash's surprise, Zak didn't argue. He just nodded and left the lounge. As soon as Zak was gone, Tash turned to Hoole. "If Zak is really sick, the cure might be in the files."

She didn't mention her other reason for wanting to decode the files: Zak had learned that Evazan was conducting his terrible experiments for someone in the Empire. It had occurred to her that the files might contain information about Imperial activities, information she could use for revenge.

Revenge was not something Tash had ever thought about before. At home on Alderaan, she had never had any enemies, and she always tried to forgive friends who accidentally hurt or upset her.

But that had been before the Empire ruined her life. In one merciless moment, the Emperor's Death Star had wiped out her friends, her family, her entire world. As the shock of the tragedy wore off, Tash's grief had started to turn to anger. Lately she had begun to think about ways of getting back at the Empire. For some time now she had been dreaming of becoming a Jedi Knight and waging a war to defeat the Empire.

But the Jedi were extinct. They had been hunted down and destroyed by the Empire. Tash knew she would have to find a different way to battle the Imperials, and she thought the files might give her a weapon. If she could decode the documents, then give them to the Rebel Alliance, she could strike a blow against the murderers who had destroyed her homeworld.

"You are right about Zak, of course," Hoole replied. "But I'm not sure how we will break this code."

"I know someone who can do it," Tash said. "Forceflow."

Hoole's face grew sterner than usual. "Tash, I know the HoloNet can be a source of entertainment and education, but I can't say I approve of the friendships you acquire. You never know whom you may be talking to. This Forceflow may be a prankster or a troublemaker."

"No, he's not!" Tash said. She stopped herself. She knew Forceflow was honest, but she also knew that Uncle Hoole would only tolerate so much arguing. "He does know a lot about codes. It can't hurt to try," she told him.

"Very well," Hoole said with a sigh. "But I insist that you immediately come to me with whatever information he gives you." He gave Tash a datadisk filled with the coded files. Returning to her cabin, Tash sat down at her computer screen.

Punching in commands, Tash tried to regain her connection to the HoloNet. She typed in her HoloNet code name, and then typed a message:

TO FORCEFLOW. I NEED YOUR HELP.

If anyone could help her, Forceflow could. He—or she—often broadcast information about illegal Imperial activities and other political messages. Forceflow was the kind of person Tash would have ignored six months ago. But six months ago her parents were alive.

Tash was sure that Forceflow was a Rebel on the run from the Empire.

GREETINGS, SEARCHER. The message flashed across the screen. GLAD YOU'RE BACK.

Tash typed quickly. NEED FILES DECODED. ALSO NEED INFORMATION ON "PROJECT STARSCREAM." MAY BE IMPERIAL DOCUMENTS.

There was a pause. Then a return message flashed: NOT SURE IT'S SAFE. IMPERIALS MAY BE MONITORING MY FREQUENCIES.

Tash was in a hurry to learn who was behind the experiments, and she wanted to know if Zak was in serious danger. She typed, THIS IS URGENT.

UPLOAD NOW. BUT IF I'M DETECTED, I'LL HAVE TO CUT OFF.

Tash inserted a datadisk into her computer and punched a key. Instantly, a data signal was beamed across the galaxy. Somewhere, on one of a hundred thousand worlds, the mysterious Forceflow was receiving her data.

Suddenly her computer emitted an electronic scream. Her screen went dark. When it came back on, the words seemed to shake on the screen.

I'M BEING SCANNED! RECEIVED PART OF YOUR FILES. WILL GET BACK TO YOU!

The message ended there.

Tash wanted to send another message. What if Forceflow needed help? If he was caught, it would be her fault.

But before she could type in another word, the door to her cabin slid open. Zak stood in the doorway. All the blood had drained from his face, and he was drenched in sweat.

"I think . . . ," he said weakly. "I think I'm not feeling well."

Then he collapsed.

CHAPTER

Less than an hour later Tash sat at her brother's bedside, watching him toss and turn in his sleep. She had cried out when he fell, which brought Hoole and Deevee running. They had quickly carried Zak to his bed.

"Isn't there anything we can do?" she asked.

Deevee replied, "There are many medical devices on board this ship, but considering the fact that Evazan was called Dr. Death, I don't think we should use them on Zak."

"What about you, Deevee? Don't you have a medical program?"

The droid shook his silver-domed head. "I have data files on the medical practices of thousands of worlds, but my own skills are limited to the first aid I learned when Master Hoole adopted you."

Hoole's rigid face softened slightly. "Tash, I'm reluctant to bring up a painful subject, but do you recall what your mother did when you were ill?"

Again Tash felt a twinge. If only her mother were here! She replied, "I don't know. I was never really sick."

"Never?" Hoole questioned.

She shook her head. "Not that I remember. I just never seemed to catch anything. But when Zak wasn't feeling well, she used to check his temperature."

Tash put her wrist against Zak's forehead. His skin was hot, and damp with perspiration. "He's burning up. I think he's got a fever, Uncle Hoole."

The Shi'ido put a hand on her shoulder. "We mustn't take chances, Tash. We are less than fifteen hours away from the Mah Dala Infirmary on the planet Gobindi."

"Infirmary?" she asked. "You mean, a hospital?"

Hoole nodded. "The Infirmary on Gobindi is said to be the finest medical facility in this part of the galaxy. It is also run by an old colleague of mine in the Imperial Biological Welfare Department."

Imperial Biological Welfare Department? Tash wanted nothing to do with Imperials.

But beside her, Zak moaned in his sleep. His temperature seemed to be rising by the minute. He was definitely ill, and any help—even Imperial help—would be welcome.

Hoole turned to his assistant droid. "Deevee, program

19

the *Shroud*'s navicomputer to take us to Gobindi immediately."

"Right away, Master Hoole." The droid hurried to set the coordinates as Hoole said, "Tash, I have some things I must do before we reach Gobindi. Please call me at once if there is any change in Zak's condition."

Tash nodded.

Alone, Tash watched her brother's fitful sleep. She couldn't help thinking that the Empire was responsible for this in some way. Minute by minute, Tash felt her anger grow, until it burned hotter than Zak's fever.

"You're going to be fine, Zak," she whispered, patting his hand. "You're going to be just fine. And I promise that somehow I'm going to make the Empire pay for this."

After a while Deevee came to replace Tash.

"We are still several hours away from Gobindi. Why don't you rest for a little while?" he said, his electronic voice imitating concern so perfectly that Tash was sure the droid felt emotions. "I have added some basic medical skills to my program, and I'm confident I can care for young Zak."

Reluctantly Tash allowed Deevee to take her place, but she did not rest. Instead she went straight to her cabin and logged onto her computer.

MESSAGE TO FORCEFLOW.

She waited. There was no response.

She decided to post a message anyway, hoping that he would pick it up soon and send a reply.

20

FORCEFLOW. I NEED INFORMATION RIGHT AWAY. WILL TRY TO CONTACT YOU AS SOON AS WE REACH THE PLANET GOBINDI. REPLY SOON!

She transmitted her message, hoping that her mysterious contact would receive it before Zak grew any sicker.

Three hours later, the *Shroud* prepared to drop out of hyperspace into the Gobindi system. Tash sat next to her uncle. He had asked her to act as his copilot, while Deevee remained by Zak's side, ready to use the new skills he had just programmed into his computer brain.

Uncle Hoole deactivated the hyperdrive, and Tash watched out the forward viewport as the stars changed from the white streaks of hyperspace to the twinkling pinpoints of realspace.

And then they were blotted out by the shadow of an Imperial Star Destroyer.

Collision alarms blared in the *Shroud*'s cockpit. Tash stifled a cry as Hoole jerked the ship's navigational stick hard to the left and the *Shroud* plunged down and away from the Destroyer. The Star Destroyer's huge, wedgelike shape cut through the fabric of space like a blade as it passed above them.

Hoole was still trying to regain control of the *Shroud* when the first laser shot streaked past them, just meters from the *Shroud*'s hull. Another shot followed, and only the Shi'ido's flight pattern saved them from becoming a ball of exploding gases.

21

"Why are they firing at us?" Tash yelled.

Hoole's voice was tight and controlled. "I don't know."

"Raise our deflector shields!" she urged.

"If I do, they will think we want to fight or escape."

Another laser shot flared nearby, even closer than the one before. "Tash," Hoole ordered, "open a comm channel. Tell them we mean no harm."

Tash activated the *Shroud*'s comm system, but before she could send her message a voice blared over the speakers.

"Attention, unidentified ship. You have been targeted as a pirate ship. Prepare to be boarded or destroyed!"

"Pirates? Why do they think we're pirates?" Tash shouted.

"Reply to their message," Hoole said with amazing calm. "Tell them we are not pirates and we will cooperate."

Once more Tash activated the *Shroud*'s comm system, but all the channels were filled with harsh static. "I think they're jamming our signal," she said.

Hoole focused on the controls but managed to mutter, "They hailed us as an unidentified ship. Aren't we broadcasting a telesponder code?"

Tash had a lot to learn about star piloting, but she knew that telesponder codes were the automatic signals all starships sent out so that other ships could identify them. The only people who didn't use telesponder codes were pirates and smugglers.

Tash searched the control console for the appropriate switch and found that it had been shut down. She realized what had happened. "Zak must have accidentally turned it off when he passed out up here." She flipped the switch. "I hope this helps."

Tash expected that it would only take a few seconds for the telesponder to begin transmitting and for someone aboard the enormous Imperial warship to receive the code. But she did not expect the Destroyer to stop firing and suddenly veer off.

The Imperial voice broadcast over their loudspeaker once again, and this time it was filled with concern. "Apologies. A mistaken transmission. You are clear to proceed."

Without another word, the Star Destroyer sliced its way along the space lane.

"What was that all about?" Tash asked.

Hoole gave the slightest shrug. "No harm was done. Let's make haste for the Gobindi system."

No harm done! Tash thought. *They could have destroyed us, and they hardly gave it a thought. The Imperials don't do anything but hurt people.*

As the *Shroud*'s sublight engines propelled them through the star system, Tash and Uncle Hoole saw three more

Star Destroyers, all bristling with weapons and cutting across the orbital paths of the Gobindi system's twelve planets.

"Four Star Destroyers," Uncle Hoole murmured to himself. "Almost a fleet. Something important must be happening in the area to attract so many ships."

But now that the *Shroud* was broadcasting its telesponder code, none of the Imperial war ships challenged them again.

Finally the *Shroud* plunged toward Gobindi, the fifth planet of the system, a massive green globe half covered in thick cloud layers. From orbit, Gobindi looked like a huge jungle.

As they approached, Tash felt the planet's gravity grab hold and draw them in quickly. Hoole handled their ship expertly, guiding it toward a growing spot of white in the thick carpet of green vegetation. "That is Mah Dala, the capital city of Gobindi," Hoole said. "I sent a message ahead to Dr. Kavafi, my colleague at the Imperial Biological Welfare Division. He is expecting us."

The *Shroud* swooped down over Mah Dala. The city seemed to be made up of many-leveled pyramids with flat tops. Elaborate bridges connected the buildings in beautifully intricate designs.

"The Gobindi are amazing architects," Tash observed.

"Were," Hoole responded. "The Gobindi themselves vanished years ago. No one knows what happened to them. The only city they left behind was Mah Dala. I've always wanted to visit the ruins here but never found the time."

"Who lives here now?" she asked.

Hoole banked the *Shroud,* headed toward a landing bay, and answered, "The Empire opened the planet up to colonization a few years ago, and many different species moved into Mah Dala. This area of space gets a lot of traffic, and the hyperspace lanes are quite close. It's something of a cosmopolitan place now, I believe. And, of course, the Imperials are here."

"Of course," Tash muttered.

The *Shroud* settled onto a landing platform that sat atop one of the flat pyramids. The minute the ship rested on its landing gear, Tash unbuckled her crash webbing and hurried back to the main lounge. Deevee was holding Zak in his mechanical arms. Her brother was wrapped in a blanket, still sweating and mumbling to himself. He looked half-awake.

"Zak?" Tash said softly. "How do you feel?"

In misery he looked up at his sister. "My head's on fire, Tash."

Hoole activated the hatchway. The door flew open, and Tash found herself looking into the concerned face of a human male about fifty years old. He had brown hair, lightly salted with gray, and warm blue eyes. He wore a brown Imperial uniform with the letters "IBWD" stitched over the left breast, and he was holding a medical datapad in one hand. Behind him stood two technicians pushing a hover-gurney.

The man looked past Tash and smiled. "Dr. Hoole. It's good to see you again."

Hoole reached forward and shook the man's hand quickly. "Dr. Kavafi. I know you are busy. Thank you for seeing to this personally."

"Think nothing of it. Let's see the patient to the Infirmary, shall we?"

He nodded to the two technicians, who quickly took Zak from Deevee's arms and laid him gently on the hover-gurney. Kavafi quickly examined Zak, then grabbed a comlink from his belt and spoke into it. "Medi-chamber six, this is Dr. Kavafi. I'm bringing in a patient with a high fever. From the looks of things, I would say it is a low-grade virus. Have the diagnostic droid standing by."

Quickly the technicians grabbed hold of the hover-gurney and pushed it toward a waiting medi-shuttle. Tash, Hoole, and Deevee followed Dr. Kavafi.

"Is he going to be all right?" Tash asked Dr. Kavafi.

The doctor smiled. "Don't worry, young lady," he said. "Everything is going to be just fine."

Tash suddenly remembered Forceflow. Had he ever replied to her message? If he did have information regarding Project Starscream, they might use it to help the doctors cure Zak.

"I, uh, forgot something," she told Hoole, then quickly turned back toward the ship.

"Hurry," Hoole ordered. "We need to get Zak to the hospital right away."

Tash leaped back into the ship and headed straight for her cabin. Inside, she powered up her computer terminal.

There was a message waiting for her. It had arrived just before their encounter with the Star Destroyer.

Tash's blood ran cold when she read the words on her computer screen.

SEARCHER, THIS IS FORCEFLOW. HAVE INFORMATION REGARDING PROJECT STARSCREAM. WHATEVER YOU DO, STAY AWAY FROM GOBINDI. STAY AWAY FROM GOBINDI!

CHAPTER 4

Tash stared at the words on the screen, hoping that somehow they would change. But they didn't.

STAY AWAY FROM GOBINDI!

Why?

What did Project Starscream have to do with Gobindi? Tash needed to communicate with Forceflow again, and quickly.

"Tash!" Uncle Hoole called from outside the ship. "Hurry!"

Hesitantly Tash powered down her computer. The message faded away.

STAY AWAY FROM GOBINDI!

Whatever Forceflow's message meant, it had come too late.

Moments later the medi-shuttle zoomed smoothly across the level tops of Mah Dala's pyramidlike stone buildings.

Tash sat at her brother's side, pressing a cool, damp cloth to his forehead. Hoole and Deevee stayed to one side, quietly talking.

Tash spared a glance away from her brother. Over Hoole's shoulder, she looked out the shuttle's viewport. Structures made of enormous stone tables, each one slightly smaller than the one beneath it, climbed into the sky. The sides of the buildings looked like massive steps, and she imagined giants using the buildings as stairways to space.

The bridges connecting the pyramids looked like tiny threads that held the stone giants together. Tash guessed that the highest of the bridges were suspended three hundred meters above the ground.

"Magnificent, aren't they?" Dr. Kavafi said with a smile. "They are called ziggurats. The Gobindi were obviously powerful builders."

"Impressive," Hoole said. "Kavafi, once we are sure Zak is recovering, I would like to make arrangements to study these ruins."

Tash felt anger prick her insides. Was Hoole planning to do anthropological research while he was here? Didn't he care about Zak?

"Indeed," Deevee added, eager to join any conversation about ancient civilizations. "I have done only preliminary work on Gobindi, but I understand that the natives

29

built these towers so that they could escape the thick jungles below. Dr. Kavafi, is it true they only lived in the highest levels of the ziggurats?''

Tash wished they would all be quiet. She had no interest in lost civilizations or architecture. All she wanted was for Zak to get better.

Beside her, Kavafi shrugged at the droid's question. ''Anthropology is Hoole's area, not mine. But that seems to be the case. However some of the ziggurats have no inner chambers at all. They are just artificial mountains. The tops of others contain many rooms and hallways, but below those levels they are mostly solid rock. There is nowhere to live down near the bottom. Apparently the jungle is too thick, and the wildlife is not always harmless.''

''The Gobindi must have been quite highly advanced scientifically, to build—''

''I'm sorry,'' Kavafi said, still monitoring Zak's vital signs. ''Perhaps we should wait until Zak here can join the conversation.''

The droid stopped talking. Tash looked at Kavafi out of the corner of her eye. That comment almost made her like him, even if he was an Imperial.

''Ah, here we are,'' Kavafi said.

Dr. Kavafi pointed out the window of the shuttle. Following his gaze, Tash found herself staring at the biggest building she had ever seen. It was shaped like the other ziggurats, but it was almost twice as large as any of the buildings around it. At the very top, Imperial engineers had built a modern steelcrete tower. The tower must have been twenty stories high, but it looked like little more than a small cap sitting atop the enormous ziggurat.

"That newer structure is the Infirmary," Kavafi explained. "Below it are the ruins of the oldest and largest ziggurat on Gobindi."

The shuttle banked smoothly and landed on top of the ziggurat. Tash stood at Zak's side as the two assistants guided the hover-gurney out of the shuttle and immediately headed toward the Infirmary.

When Tash stepped out of the shuttle, she felt as though she'd walked right into a steam bath. The air was moist and hot, and so thick she could almost taste it as she breathed in. In moments she and Hoole were both sweating from the heat, but because the air was so moist, their perspiration didn't dry. Their clothing soon stuck to their skin. Even Deevee appeared uncomfortable as they hurried across the top of the ziggurat to the Infirmary.

"This humidity is extraordinary," the droid said. "I can already feel my outer covering starting to rust."

Kavafi nodded. "And this is a good day. Most days are hotter and wetter than this."

Tash ignored the heat, searching for signs of danger. But only the wide flat surface of the ziggurat stretched out before them, with the gray tower rising above. What had Forceflow's message meant? Was he warning her about Imperials? Was there some other danger?

Suddenly Zak moaned in his sleep. "Mom." Tash bit her lip. Zak's face was still bloodless and even in sleep, he looked miserable.

"Halt!"

Tash looked up.

They were surrounded by Imperial stormtroopers.

CHAPTER

There were at least two squads of stormtroopers in white armor standing at the wide doorways to the Infirmary. The blank masks of their helmets looked as terrifying and impersonal as the Empire itself.

One of the stormtroopers raised a weapon, and Tash thought he was going to open fire. But instead, the weapon merely glowed briefly as the trooper pointed it at the newcomers.

"All clear," he reported. "Energy scan reveals no weapons."

"You are clear to proceed," another trooper told them, clearing a path to the door.

"For a hospital, you seem quite well guarded," Hoole observed.

Kavafi looked almost embarrassed. "Unfortunate but

necessary. This star system has experienced increased pirate activity in the past few weeks. Smugglers and spacejackers trying to steal medical supplies. We've had to expand our security."

They passed the stormtroopers and reached the front of the gray tower. Over the doors, the letters "IBWD" had been set in black onyx.

"Welcome," Kavafi said, "to the Imperial Biological Welfare Division."

Tash followed closely as Zak was carried through the doors of the steelcrete tower. The Infirmary's ground floor was a vast lobby filled with turbolift banks and people scurrying to and fro. Most of them were human, and most of them wore Imperial uniforms, but there was a smattering of alien species. Since the Empire rarely employed anyone but humans, Tash guessed that the aliens must be patients seeking treatment at the Infirmary.

They reached a turbolift and hastily pushed Zak's hover-gurney inside. Kavafi turned to the lift's control panel and said, "Floor ten. Override any other floor calls."

"Acknowledged," said a mechanical voice, and the turbolift rose quickly.

While most turbolifts still used a simple push-button system, Tash had seen many lifts like this one before. The lift car itself was actually a class-four service droid. It responded to simple voice commands and was programmed to shuttle occupants up and down the turbolift shaft.

The droid-powered lift took them up to the tenth floor, where Zak was moved into a medi-chamber with calm efficiency. For a few moments the room was a blur of motion as technicians took samples of his blood, hooked up monitors to his chest and forehead, and prepared medication.

Kavafi held up an enormous needle and examined a dark fluid within it. "What's that?" Tash asked nervously.

"Just something to help him sleep," Kavafi said. "Sometimes sleep is the best medicine of all."

He bent down and prepared to insert the needle. Tash shuddered as the needle slipped under his skin. As soon as he'd given Zak the injection, Kavafi checked the monitors, nodded to himself, and sighed.

"Is he going to be all right?" Hoole asked. Despite the fact that his own nephew now lay in a hospital bed, Hoole's voice was as steady and businesslike as ever.

"Oh, yes," Kavafi replied confidently. "We will run some tests to be sure, but the early indications are that Zak has a strain of influenza."

"I thought you said he had a virus," Tash replied.

Kavafi smiled patiently. Tash realized that he was trying to make her feel comfortable. She appreciated it, but her brother was ill, and she was standing inside an Imperial facility guarded by Imperial soldiers and run by Imperial doctors. Even if they were Hoole's friends, she was anything but comfortable.

"Influenza *is* a virus," Kavafi explained. "There are millions of viruses throughout the galaxy. Each one of them causes different problems, sometimes quite serious ones."

Tash swallowed. "Is—Is he going to—"

"No, no!" Kavafi said, putting a hand on her shoulder. "He will be fine. Usually a person's body can fight off the virus after a little while. Would you like to *see* what is causing your brother to be ill?"

Tash was surprised. "You mean, you can see it?"

"Not with your eye, but with this." Kavafi picked up a visor off the desk. The lenses were deep red, with tiny control switches mounted on the sides. "This is an electroscope. It allows you to see objects a thousand times smaller than the tip of a hydrospanner. Right now it's programmed to find and locate viruses. Here."

He pointed to a small glass plate sitting on a counter. The plate contained a sample of red fluid. Tash stared at the small drop of fluid as she put on the visor and felt on the side panel for the power switch. When she flipped it, the medi-chamber vanished. Tash found herself peering into a world of swirling red currents. In the center of the currents was a large mass that moved and wriggled as though it was alive. Suddenly six ominous-looking creatures swam into view. They had large, faceless heads covered with thick strands of what looked like hair. Their bodies tapered into long, thin tails that they used to swim about in the red fluid. Without pause the six creatures swarmed the wriggling mass. Five of the creatures succeeded in piercing its membrane. They forced themselves inside the mass, eating away at it.

As Tash watched, the five creatures suddenly trembled, and then they split apart, becoming ten organisms. And then twenty, and then forty! They were replicating faster than Tash could count them.

The sixth wriggling creature, the one that hadn't succeeded in getting inside the floating mass, turned, and with a sudden surge, lunged right at Tash.

"Ah!" Tash jumped back. Then she remembered she was wearing the electroscope. She was looking at the fluid on a small glass plate, magnified thousands of times.

"Startling, isn't it?" she heard Kavafi say. "Those tiny organisms are what make living beings sick. They invade the body and begin to reproduce, taking over the body's living cells."

Tash watched as more of the viruses swam into view. They seemed to be searching for something. "Are they fatal?"

"Sometimes," the doctor admitted. "But since the virus feeds off its living host, it doesn't usually want to kill it. Sometimes viruses can live and reproduce inside an animal or person for years, causing all kinds of terrible illnesses."

Tash removed the electroscope. "How do you get them?

I mean, they're too small to travel from one place to another.''

The doctor nodded. ''Viruses get around in all kinds of ways. Sometimes touching an infected person can give you the virus, or drinking infected water. Some viruses even float through the air.''

A medical droid entered the room carrying a tray that had two needles on it. Kavafi picked up one of the needles. ''Hoole, I'm afraid I'm going to have to ask you and your niece to endure an injection.''

''For what purpose?'' the Shi'ido asked. ''We are not sick.''

Kavafi shrugged. ''Just a precaution. You and your niece may have caught the virus that Zak has, and I want to stop it before it has time to take hold in your system.'' He held the needle out toward Hoole.

Hoole stuck one long, thin arm out from beneath his blue robe. Kavafi quickly and expertly stuck the needle into the Shi'ido's arm and squeezed until all the fluid had been injected.

''Your turn,'' he said cheerily to Tash.

''I never catch anything,'' she insisted. ''I never get sick.''

''Better safe than sorry,'' he replied.

Reluctantly Tash held out her arm. She felt a quick prick as the needle poked beneath her skin, then a slight tugging as the fluid was injected into her bloodstream. For a moment the injection felt hot and stinging. Then the pain passed.

"There we are," Kavafi said cheerily. "Now all your worries are over. I will be right back."

The minute Kavafi left the room, Tash turned to the Shi'ido and whispered, "Uncle Hoole! I think something's wrong here!"

Hoole raised his eyebrows. "What?"

"Just before we left the *Shroud,* I got a message from Forceflow. He warned us not to come to Gobindi!"

Hoole furrowed his eyebrows. "Tash, I appreciate your concern. But why should we change our plans, based on a warning from a person you have never actually met?"

Tash searched for a reply. "He's always helped me before."

Hoole said, "He is meddling in affairs he cannot possibly understand. I cannot permit you to run your life based on mysterious messages sent over the HoloNet."

"But this is an Imperial base!" Tash argued. "There are stormtroopers here!"

Hoole sighed. "I know how you feel about the Empire, and you have a right to be angry. But you have to understand that the government has officers, soldiers, and fleets of ships all across the galaxy. Most of the time they are just beings going about their daily business. If you think that every time you see stormtroopers you have uncovered a wicked Imperial plot, you will go insane with worry.

You must learn to control your suspicion, or it will control you.''

"But—"

"Tash, please." Hoole looked at her sternly. "I have known Dr. Kavafi for years. He is a good scientist, dedicated to improving the lives of species-kind. We are in no danger."

The tone in Hoole's voice told Tash that she should not continue the argument. She crossed her arms as if to hold in her frustration.

As she did, she felt a small pain in her left arm. She touched the tender spot where she had received the injection. "I think your friend bruised me with that needle," she muttered.

Dr. Kavafi returned just as Zak moaned loudly in his sleep. Tash reached down and wiped the sweat off his forehead. "Why is he so hot?"

"That's the human way of fighting off disease. Most viruses cannot take extreme heat, so your body automatically raises its temperature to fight back."

Tash couldn't help thinking the worst. "But what happens if this virus actually *likes* the heat?"

Kavafi raised his eyebrows in surprise. "Well, that is a very interesting scenario. It would cause great problems for the victim, I think. Let's just hope you never encounter a virus like that."

Hoole asked, "Kavafi, is there anything else we can do?"

The doctor shook his head. "No. He will sleep for a while now. We will need to run some tests on Zak to make sure there is nothing else wrong. My best advice is for you to go out and refresh yourselves. His sedative should wear off in about an hour."

"I'm not leaving," Tash said. "What if he wakes up early?"

"I will stay with him," Uncle Hoole decided. "Tash, I want you and Deevee to find a cantina and get something to eat."

"I'm not hungry," Tash replied.

"Then at least go for a walk," the Shi'ido insisted. "Zak will be fine."

"I will take you back down," Kavafi offered. "I have business below, myself."

Tash didn't want to leave her brother, but Hoole would hear no argument. Finally she and Deevee followed Kavafi out of the room and back to the lifts. They got in and Kavafi said, "Lobby."

"Does this lift go down into the ziggurat itself?" Deevee asked excitedly.

"No, no," the doctor replied. "As I said before, some of the ziggurats have no rooms or chambers. This is one of them. I'm afraid it's just an enormous mountain of stone."

The turbolift descended with a soft whoosh, and the doors opened onto the Infirmary lobby. Tash and Deevee stepped off, but Kavafi stayed behind.

"Aren't you getting off?" Tash asked. "This is the bottom floor, isn't it?"

Kavafi paused. "Oh, of course. But I forgot my datapad upstairs. I will have to go back and get it." The doors closed.

Tash and Deevee walked out of the lobby to the edge of the ziggurat and looked down. The sides of the tower stuck out below them in jagged steps that were eventually lost in hazy clouds. Nearby, they saw a footbridge connecting this ziggurat to several others. It seemed stable, and soon they were walking along the path, hundreds of meters above the ground.

Deevee had begun a lecture on the number of lost civilizations in the galaxy, including the Massassi of Yavin Four and the Ysanna of Ossus, but Tash wasn't listening. Her eye had fallen on a shape on the bridge ahead of them. As they closed the distance, she expected its shape to become clearer . . . but even as close as ten meters away it looked like a blob. Its center appeared hard and somewhat firm, but around the edges, the greenish shape oozed and pulsed. Although it was lying fairly flat, the blob was slightly larger than a human being, and it had spread across the bridge in a pile of steaming ooze.

"What's that?" she asked. "Is it alive?"

Deevee didn't answer. He didn't have to.

The blob surged toward them.

CHAPTER 6

Tash and Deevee both scrambled backward as the blob lunged forward and landed heavily on the spot where they had been standing. The impact caused the creature to flatten out briefly, but then it gathered itself up for another spring. Rolls of squishy green gel rippled across its surface.

"Deevee, what is it?" Tash cried.

"I'm familiar with more than fifteen billion forms of life in the galaxy," the droid replied with a hint of panic in his electronic voice, "but I've never seen anything like it."

The blob made no sound, except for the slimy slap of its wriggling, fatty skin on the surface of the bridge. Then it sprang again. Tash jumped backward, but this time

Deevee was too slow. The oozing creature landed heavily against his legs, sending the droid clattering to the floor of the bridge.

"Help! Help!" Deevee tried to pry himself loose as the blob began to creep up his silver legs.

"Get off him!" Tash yelled.

Tash never knew where the man came from. He seemed to appear out of nowhere. His flight suit was clean but worn, and he wore pilot's gloves that were frayed around the edges. His features were sharp and his face looked young but very serious. The man wore a blaster at his hip, but he kept it holstered. Without saying a word he kicked the blob with his booted foot. The blob did not react, but the man's boot sank into the wriggling skin up to the ankle. He grunted and pried himself free.

"Use your blaster!" Tash suggested.

"Don't hit me!" Deevee added.

The man ignored them both. He grabbed the upper edge of the blob in his gloved hands and yanked hard. The ooze peeled away from Deevee's metallic surface. But that only seemed to make the blob angry. It let go of its sticky grip on the droid and turned on their rescuer. Two squishy ropes of ooze—almost like arms—suddenly grabbed hold of the man.

"By the Force!" he yelled in surprise as he lost his balance. He staggered backward toward the edge of the high bridge. "I could use some help," he grunted as he tried to lift the blob up over the bridge's guardrail.

Tash hurried to his side, but the man said, "Don't touch it! Get the droid. And hurry!" The creature's oozing limbs had almost crept up to his shoulders.

Deevee rose stiffly to his feet and shuffled over as fast as his servos would carry him. "I am not programmed to handle this," he muttered as he grabbed hold of the blob. He tried to lift it. "By the Maker, this creature is heavier than a human!" Deevee's computer brain automatically transferred more power to his upper servos, and he and the newcomer lifted the blob up and over the guardrail.

"Okay, drop it!" the man ordered, bracing himself against the rail.

Deevee let go, and the blob dropped a few feet. Two thick strands of ooze still clung to the man's shoulders, but as the blob's own weight dragged it down, the ooze ropes stretched thinner and thinner.

"Hold on!" Tash shouted.

"Good . . . advice!" the man grunted, pulling back against the weight of the blob. At last the strands of ooze snapped. The blob dropped. Tash watched as the creature shrank away beneath them, finally disappearing into the jungle steam. She looked at the man, who was still panting from his efforts.

"Thanks!" was all she could manage.

"Yes, indeed!" Deevee added, picking himself up. His legs were covered in a sticky trail of green slime. "That creature would have turned me into scrap! How fortunate that you happened to be nearby."

"Yeah," the man replied. "Lucky. Did that thing touch you?" he asked Tash.

"No. Why? Are they poisonous?" Tash asked.

"Not poisonous." The man cast a nervous glance around, and held up his hands. His gloves were covered in ooze. He carefully removed them and dropped them over the side of the bridge. Tash watched them flutter toward the ground, hundreds of meters below.

Tash pointed to the weapon holstered at the man's hip. "Why didn't you just blast it?"

At that moment, a hovercar whizzed by. On its side panel, Tash caught a glimpse of the official seal of the Empire. The car zoomed away from them and toward the medical tower.

The man nodded after it. "That's why. Using a blaster might bring a different kind of bug. The *Imperial* kind." As he said this the man watched Tash closely. She had the feeling that he was trying to judge her reaction to his comment about the Empire.

"What was that thing?" she asked, looking over the side. The cries of jungle creatures floated up from below.

The man did not take his eyes off her. "As far as I know, they don't have names. *Blob* is as good a word as any, I guess. They just started creeping out of the jungle a few weeks ago. Before that no one had seen them. But then, these jungles are full of the unexpected."

"And they are allowed to roam at will?" Deevee asked indignantly.

"They seemed pretty harmless," the man replied. "And they're hard to stop. That sticky ooze allows them to climb up walls and hang from ceilings. Even a fall from this height probably didn't kill that one."

Tash shuddered. She imagined the blob splattering onto the forest floor beneath them, then slowly gathering itself back up and making the long climb back up the ziggurat.

Deevee was still in a huff. "Why, then, the local imperials should do something about them. It's an outrage."

Again the man studied Tash's reaction as he scoffed, "Imperials. What do you expect from them?"

"My name's Tash," she said. "This is DV-9, or Deevee for short."

The man shook her hand. "I'm Wedge Antilles. Where are you headed?"

Tash shrugged. "We were just going for a walk around the city. These pyramids—ziggurats—are pretty impressive."

Wedge nodded. "Listen, how about if I give you a quick walking tour?"

Tash started to reply, "Thanks, but I don't think we—"

"You'll need a guide," Wedge interrupted. "All the bridges between the ziggurats can be confusing. Sometimes I think it would take a Jedi to navigate Mah Dala."

The word was like a magnet that drew Tash's attention straight to Wedge.

"You know about the Jedi?" she asked breathlessly.

47

The corners of Wedge's mouth turned up in a slight smile. "I've heard of them."

"I've always wanted to be one," Tash said. She turned to Deevee. "I suppose it wouldn't hurt to have a guide."

But the man's manner had triggered Deevee's cautious caretaker programming. "I'm afraid Tash's uncle would not want her to roam a new city with a complete stranger."

Wedge Antilles sighed. "Oh, well. I'm the best guide you'll find around here. I could have shown you some out-of-the-way examples of Gobindi architecture and ancient culture that you'd never find on your own, but if that's how you feel—"

"Culture?" the droid replied with sudden enthusiasm. "Well, I'm sure Master Hoole would not want Tash to miss an educational opportunity. Lead on, Master Antilles."

Wedge led them across the bridge and into the next ziggurat. This one was bustling with activity. The halls inside the flat-topped pyramid were high and wide, with many side corridors and lifts rising up and down. *If all the buildings are this well populated,* Tash thought, *Mah Dala must be a fairly crowded place.*

The beings inside the ziggurat came from every corner of the galaxy. Many were human, but there were also large numbers of furry Bothans, Twi'leks with skull tendrils draped across their shoulders, and dozens of other species walking, crawling, or writhing about. Tash recalled what

Hoole had said: The original Gobindi had vanished, and many other species had filled the city they left behind.

They stopped and sat on a bench in the middle of a central plaza as the crowd hurried past.

"This isn't much of a cultural experience," Deevee sniffed. "Crowd-watching is for amateur anthropologists."

Tash ignored him. She was more interested in the man who had saved their lives. "Are you from Gobindi?" she asked.

Wedge shook his head. "No. I'm just visiting some friends. I've been here for several weeks, though. Long enough to know the city pretty well. Actually I only planned to stay a few days. But of course with the blockade and all—"

"Blockade?" Tash interrupted. "What blockade?"

Yet again the man's eyes seemed to peer inside Tash's head. Tash had the distinct impression that this encounter with Wedge was no accident. It was a strange sensation, but Tash often had unexplainable feelings about people and events. Lately she'd learned to trust her intuition.

Wedge spoke matter-of-factly. "The blockade of the Gobindi system. According to the Imperial news broadcasts, pirate activity has gotten so bad that the Empire has sent a fleet of Star Destroyers to deal with the problem."

"We saw them," Tash responded. "But we didn't see any pirate ships."

49

Wedge snorted. "No one's ever seen any pirates here. But that doesn't matter to the Empire. They've still ordered all ships to be grounded until they've had time to hunt down the criminals. So everyone's stuck here. No one has come or gone from Gobindi in almost three weeks."

Deevee spoke up. "You must be mistaken, sir. We just arrived on Gobindi. How is that possible if there is a blockade?"

Wedge raised an eyebrow. "Only Imperials have been allowed to leave or arrive."

So that's what he's after, Tash thought. *He's trying to figure out if we're Imperials!*

"We're *not* Imperials," she replied hotly.

"But your ship was allowed to land—" Wedge replied.

"We're not Imperials!" she repeated. Wedge raised his eyebrows in surprise. Even Tash was surprised at how angry she sounded. She blushed. She felt foolish, not only for yelling, but for revealing her feelings to this man. She had no idea who he was.

But even so, Tash felt a strong urge that seemed to say, *Trust him.*

Caught between these two feelings, Tash said nothing.

"So, what brings you to Gobindi?" Wedge asked.

"My brother's sick," she replied. "They're examining him at the Infirmary."

The man's face darkened. He clenched his jaw and said, "Listen, I'm going to tell you something, even though it

50

might be a mistake. For all I know you could be the daughter of some high-level Imperial officer and you could get me in a lot of trouble. But . . ."

The fear in his voice made Tash's hair stand on end. "What?" she asked.

He nodded in the direction of the Infirmary. "In the past few weeks, no one has come out of there alive."

CHAPTER

"What do you mean no one's come out of the Infirmary alive?" Tash cried.

But at that moment a siren sounded shrilly in their ears. It was followed by a white-paneled hovercar that swooped into the plaza, scattering the crowds of pedestrians. A squad of stormtroopers leaped out of the back before it even stopped. With military precision the troopers singled out a specific being in the startled crowd. Tash saw that the creature—with its green skin, large purple eyes, and narrow snout—was a Rodian. Four of the troopers pounced on him. The leader of the stormtrooper squad activated a loudspeaker built into his armor:

ATTENTION, CITIZENS OF MAH DALA. THE BEING WE ARE TAKING INTO CUSTODY HAS BEEN IDENTIFIED AS A SUSPECTED

The stormtroopers dragged the Rodian kicking and screaming to the hovercar. "I'm not a pirate! I'm not a pirate!" the Rodian yelled. But the troopers ignored him and tossed him into the waiting vehicle, then jumped in behind him. The lead trooper paused only to attach a large data screen to a nearby wall. Then he, too, slipped into the vehicle. Its sirens wailing, the Imperial hovercar slid quickly away.

"What was that all about?" Tash asked of her new companion. But Wedge had vanished.

Tash and Deevee walked over and joined the crowd that had gathered around the data screen. The flat electronic device displayed the words "WANTED FOR PIRACY." Underneath those words were four images. One was of the Rodian that had just been captured. A digital red X had been drawn through his image. But the other three images were of suspects still at large. Tash recognized the furred face of a Bothan, and two humans.

One of the humans was Wedge Antilles.

"Oh, dear," Deevee said with a start.

"I don't believe it," Tash said. "Why would a space pirate save us from that blob?"

"He did say he had been trapped here by the blockade," Deevee pointed out.

Tash still didn't believe it. Maybe it was his mention of

the Jedi, but she had a feeling that Wedge had a good heart, and she had learned to trust her feelings.

"What do you think he meant about the Infirmary?"

The droid shook his metallic head. "I can't imagine. After all, it is the finest facility of its kind, and it is run by a friend of Master Hoole's."

That did not make Tash feel any better. She already had suspicions about Uncle Hoole. "I think we should go check on Zak. Right now."

Tash didn't wait for Deevee to respond. She sprang to action and hurried back to the suspended bridge. On the way, she tried to make sense of everything that had happened. First the mysterious Wedge Antilles appeared out of nowhere to save them from a weird blob creature, and then told them that no one but Imperials had been allowed on Gobindi in weeks. And yet, Tash reminded herself, Uncle Hoole made only one comm transmission and got clearance for them to land. And the Imperial in charge of the Infirmary was an old friend of Uncle Hoole's.

A thought sent icy chills down Tash's spine. Did Uncle Hoole have connections with the Empire?

She and Zak had been traveling with Hoole for six months, but their Shi'ido uncle had never clearly explained what he did. All they knew was that Hoole was an anthropologist and that he visited different planets to study alien cultures. As Zak had once pointed out, they didn't even know Uncle Hoole's first name!

For all she knew, her uncle could be an Imperial agent.

If that's the case, Tash thought, *then he's no uncle of mine.*

Tash reached the Infirmary slightly out of breath. The hot Gobindi climate made even the slightest exertion difficult, and her sore arm had become stiff. She touched her bruise.

Something was wrong.

She rolled up her sleeve. The bruise had become a brown lump, and the skin there was dry and rough. Whatever Kavafi had given her had caused some sort of reaction.

Just as one of the turbolift doors opened, Deevee caught up to her, his gyros straining from the effort.

"Tash Arranda!" he scolded as they rode up the lift together. "How do you expect me to function as your caretaker if you continually run off like that!"

"Sorry, Deevee, but we need to make sure Zak is all right."

"I'm quite sure Zak is in good hands," the droid replied. "Dr. Kavafi is an expert in his field, and after all, Master Hoole would only bring Zak to a first-rate medical facility."

The turbolift door opened, and Tash found herself staring into the face of Dr. Kavafi. His face broke into a warm smile. "Tash, you're back from your walk so soon?"

"Um, yes. I want to see my brother," she said, slipping past him and starting down the hall.

"Wait!" Kavafi said, catching up to her. "I'm afraid you won't be able to—"

"I want to see him anyway," Tash interrupted. She had been raised to respect adults, but her concern for her brother overwhelmed her. Besides, it was hard for her to respect someone in an Imperial uniform, even if he was a doctor. She continued her march down the hall.

"Wait!" Kavafi called after her.

Tash reached the door to Zak's medi-chamber with Kavafi running to catch up with her. "If you will only listen to—"

Tash activated the automatic door and stepped into the room.

The bed was empty. Zak was gone.

CHAPTER 8

"Where's my brother?" Tash demanded.

Kavafi held out his hands to try to calm Tash. "Now, young lady, I tried to tell you that—"

"What have you done with him?"

"What is going on here?" Uncle Hoole appeared in the doorway.

"They've done something to Zak," Tash said. "They've taken him somewhere."

"Of course they have," Uncle Hoole replied. "I'm the one who authorized it."

"You know where he is?" Tash said.

"Of course I do."

"Can I see him?" she asked suspiciously.

Dr. Kavafi looked bewildered. "Of course you can see him. But he's at the other end of the hall. This way."

Tash reddened with embarrassment. She had imagined that Zak had been taken away to some chamber of horrors and subjected to bizarre experiments.

Instead Kavafi led her into a sterile white room brilliantly lit with glowpanels. In the center of the room was a large tank filled with greenish liquid. A medical technician in a crisp white uniform monitored the tank, making small adjustments. Inside the tank, Zak floated peacefully. He was hooked up to an air mask that allowed him to breathe while floating in the fluid, but otherwise, he looked very relaxed and alert. He even waved to Tash.

"A bacta tank," Deevee said. "He should heal quickly there."

Tash was surprised. Bacta was the galactic cure-all. It helped to heal wounds, stop infections, and regenerate damaged tissue. If Kavafi was treating Zak with bacta, he really was trying to cure him.

The medical technician finished adjusting the flow of bacta into the tank and then left the room with a polite nod.

Kavafi said, "It seemed the quickest way to treat his infection. I think this should kill the virus. I expect him to make a full recovery from the *influenza necrosi*."

Relief flooded through Tash. All she could do was repeat what she heard. "Full recovery? *Influenza necrosi?*"

Kavafi looked at his datapad. "That's right. We diagnosed it almost immediately and gave him the appropriate medicine. It is a fairly common illness and no danger as

58

long as it is treated," he concluded. "Once he is out of the tank, the only aftereffect may be a slight skin rash from the virus that should go away in a few days."

"Now, Tash, I think you owe Dr. Kavafi an explanation and apology for your behavior," Hoole said firmly.

Tash felt her cheeks flush again. Kavafi smiled, but she could hardly meet his eyes. "I'm sorry, doctor. It's just that I heard someone"—without knowing why, she didn't want to mention Wedge by name—"I heard some people talking in the plaza. They sort of suggested that . . . that some strange things were going on in the Infirmary."

Kavafi sighed. He looked around and said quietly, "Tash, I hope you are not too young to understand this, but working for the Empire is not always rewarding." Tash's ears perked up. She was definitely not too young to understand *this*.

Kavafi continued. "There are people who oppose the Emperor and the government. They start rumors, they spread lies. But I joined the Imperial medical staff because the Empire has the money and resources that let me treat patients in the way they deserve. Now, I don't know whether or not some of the other things you may have heard about the Empire are true, but I can promise you that I run the Infirmary as a top-notch research and medical facility. Our job here is to cure patients, and that is what we do."

After only a moment's hesitation, Tash replied, "I understand. I'm sorry to have caused a scene."

The doctor winked. "Quite all right. Nice to see some-one who cares so much about her family."

Hoole said, "Now that that is settled, Deevee and I need to return to the *Shroud*. Tash, will you stay with Zak until he is released from the bacta tank?"

"Sure," she replied.

Hoole started to leave, then turned back and said qui-etly, "And please do not make any trouble."

Tash watched Hoole depart. She felt a sudden pain stab up through her arm. She could feel the lump there start to swell.

"Dr. Kavafi?" she asked. "Will you have a look at this?"

She rolled up her sleeve. The brown lump had grown uglier and larger. It was already a few centimeters wide, and thin brown veins ran down its sides and into her skin.

"Hmmm." Dr. Kavafi picked up an electroscope and examined the bruise. "It looks as though you've had a reaction to the injection I gave you. But it is nothing seri-ous. How do you feel?"

"All right," she said. "A little tired and hot."

The doctor chuckled. "Gobindi will do that to you. I wouldn't worry about that bump. It should go away soon enough."

Tash watched the doctor as he put away the visor. The warnings she had received still echoed in her head, and she wondered if she could trust him. Maybe he had injected her with something. He could have given her some sort of drug. . . .

Tash stopped herself. He had given Hoole the same injection. He and Hoole were friends, and Hoole was fine.

"I have to go check on several other patients." Kavafi pointed to a computer terminal built into the medi-chamber wall. "Tash, while you are waiting, why don't you look at a rundown of our research program? You can see a complete presentation of the Infirmary's goals."

Tash shrugged. "Okay."

At the computer terminal, Kavafi punched in a code and the computer displayed a description of the Infirmary. Above the display, the initials "IBWD" appeared. Below the initials were the words "WELCOME TO THE IMPERIAL BIO-LOGICAL WELFARE DIVISION."

"Enjoy yourself," he said as he left the bacta chamber.

As Kavafi left, Tash began to punch absentmindedly through the computerized tour. Most of the commentary was about the benefits of Imperial research and the wise Imperial scientists who were devoted to improving life for all species.

"Yeah, right," Tash muttered. "Except on Alderaan," she said, thinking of the Empire's destruction of her homeworld.

Disgusted, she slapped the controls to wipe the lies off the screen. A moment later the computer exited the tour program and returned to the main menu. The screen went dark except for the command "ENTER PASSWORD" followed by ten blank squares. Tash was about to call for Kavafi's help, then decided not to.

Uncle Hoole had told her she was looking for conspiracies where they didn't exist. He was probably right. But she had nothing to lose by typing the word that came into her head.

Tash looked around. No one was watching her.

She typed in the letters "S-T-A-R-S-C-R-E-A-M."

The screen remained blank. Tash was just about to cancel the entry and start again when an image popped into the center of the screen. Tash's heart skipped a beat—until she recognized the same image she'd seen before. She was looking at the familiar display of the Infirmary with the letters "IBWD" appearing at the top.

But when Tash looked more closely, her throat tightened. Underneath those large letters, the text no longer read, IMPERIAL BIOLOGICAL WELFARE DIVISION.

Now it read, IMPERIAL BIOLOGICAL WEAPONS DIVISION.

CHAPTER

Tash read the words over and over. Biological weapons.

Biological *weapons*.

She shuddered. The lump on her arm throbbed and stretched. Tash almost thought she saw it quiver under her sleeve.

The medical technician came into the room, and Tash quickly hit the computer's Escape button, wiping the image clear.

She walked back to the bacta tank in which Zak was being treated. He smiled at her again; then he put two hands together and laid his head on them as though napping.

This is a bore, he was saying.

Tash had no way to mime her own message. She looked to make sure the medical technician was not watching, and mouthed the words, *Zak, we're caught inside a biological weapons plant!*

Inside the bacta tank Zak raised his eyebrows and shook his head. He didn't understand. Tash mouthed the words slowly.

Bi-o-lo-gi-cal weapons!

Again Zak did not understand. Tash decided to try a different, simpler word.

Tash pointed to a picture on the wall. It was a plain piece of artwork, a painting someone had done of a starfield. She put a finger on the painting itself and pointed to one star in the starfield. Zak nodded vigorously that he understood. A star.

Tash walked back to the tank, put her hands on her head, and opened her mouth wide as if she were yelling.

Star. Scream.

Starscream.

Zak nodded again. He understood.

Tash spread her hands wide, trying to cover the entire room, the entire Infirmary.

Over the air mask, Zak's eyes grew as wide as saucers.

The Infirmary was connected to Project Starscream.

Tash knew Zak understood. She motioned to Zak to remain calm. She would be back as soon as she could.

Tash hurried to the turbolifts, passing Dr. Kavafi in the hall. "Tash, where are you going?"

"I'll be back!" she said. "I need something from the ship!"

"Lobby," she said as soon as she had stepped into the lift. As she rode down, Tash suddenly felt so dizzy she had to lean against a wall for support.

They had gotten the name *Project Starscream* from the *Shroud*'s computer files. Forceflow had suggested that Starscream and the planet Gobindi were connected. And now she knew for sure the code name *Starscream* was a password into secret files inside the Infirmary.

And the Infirmary was run by Hoole's friend.

Tash needed to talk to Forceflow now more than ever.

Exiting the Infirmary, Tash walked passed the stormtroopers and out onto the top of the ziggurat. How to get back to the ship?

"Excuse me," she said to one of the troopers. She tried not to sound nervous. The trooper had no reason to think that she was anything other than a thirteen-year-old girl who needed help.

"Yeah?" the trooper asked. His voice sounded flat and filtered through his mask.

"Are there any shuttles back to the landing dock? I need to get back to my uncle's ship."

The trooper checked his chronometer. "No shuttles for another twenty minutes."

Tash didn't want to wait that long.

Since the ziggurat on which she stood was the highest

in the city, Tash could see the landing docks in the distance. Four bridges separated her from the ship.

She hurried for the first bridge. As soon as she was out of the stormtroopers' sight, she started to run.

Tash wasn't as athletic as her younger brother, but she was in good shape, so it surprised her when, after she'd passed through a second ziggurat and crossed a second bridge, her chest started to heave and her clothes to dampen with sweat. She stopped and leaned against a guardrail.

Must be the heat, she thought.

The sweat had also begun to make her itch. Her left arm felt a little numb.

Tash slowed her pace and continued to the landing dock. She noticed that the platform was crowded with starships. Tash guessed that they had been grounded by the blockade.

Reaching the *Shroud,* Tash punched in the access code and slipped inside the hatchway.

"Hello!" she called out, expecting both Hoole and Deevee to be there. But she only found Deevee working at his computer on the codes for Evazan's files.

"Hello, Tash," the droid said. "I did not expect you to return to the ship so soon." He was focused on the computer screen.

"Any luck breaking the code?" she asked.

Deevee's voice was clipped. "No. As I said before,

much as I hate to admit it, this code is far too complex for my programming.''

''Then why do you keep trying?'' she asked.

The droid shrugged. ''If I had a cipher droid, I would make use of its talents. If I had a protocol droid, I would request its assistance. But I do not. I only have my own programming, so I use it to the best of my abilities.''

Deevee stopped, pressed a button, and the screen went blank. ''I believe I am done for now. I must go and see how Zak is doing.''

''I'll come back as soon as I can,'' Tash said.

''No, Tash,'' Deevee said. ''Master Hoole's instructions were that should you come back to the ship, you should wait here until we return.''

''Right,'' she replied as Deevee slipped out the door.

Tash passed through the main lounge and entered her cabin. Dropping into the chair at her computer, she powered on and tried to catch a link to the HoloNet. She wanted to talk to Forceflow. Whoever he was, he obviously knew something about Gobindi.

HOLONET ACCESS DENIED.

The signal appeared on her computer screen. She typed in, RETRY.

HOLONET ACCESS DENIED.

Tash typed in a command, searching for the cause.

ALL OFFWORLD TRANSMISSIONS PROHIBITED BY ORDER OF THE IMPERIAL GOVERNMENT. DUE TO INCREASED PIRATE ACTIVITIES IN

THE SECTOR, THE IMPERIAL STAR FLEET HAS ORDERED ALL INTER-
PLANETARY TRANSMISSIONS IN THIS SECTOR STOPPED WHILE THEY
SEARCH FOR ILLEGAL SIGNALS.

*What's going on? No interplanetary travel. No commu-
nications. The Empire has completely cut Gobindi off from
the rest of the galaxy, and no one seems to notice.*

She typed in more commands, trying to find a way
around the jamming. She was so focused on her efforts,
that she didn't hear the hatchway open a second time.

She didn't hear her own door open.

And she never saw the figure that crept up behind her
until it was too late.

CHAPTER

10

A shadow fell across her computer screen, and Tash started. She turned around and found Wedge standing in her room. Behind him stood two other figures: One was a human with a scar running from the corner of his left eye, across the bridge of his nose, and down to the right side of his jaw. The other was a Bothan, a humanoid with blue fur that ruffled nervously.

They were the pirates Tash had seen on the data screen. She backed against the wall of her room. She was trapped.

"Tash, don't be afraid," Wedge said calmly. "We're not here to hurt you."

"What do you want? Stay away from me," she said thickly. Her heart had begun to beat rapidly.

"We're not going to hurt you," Wedge repeated. "In fact, we need your help."

"You're pirates!" she snapped.

Wedge shook his head. "We're not pirates. We're Rebels." Wedge pointed to his two companions. "We were spying on Imperial activities here in Mah Dala when the Empire clamped down and blockaded the system. Now we're stuck."

"Why are you telling me this?" she asked.

"I know I'm taking a risk," Wedge said, "but we're running out of options. The Empire knows we're here. They've already captured one of our group." Tash remembered the Rodian. "It's only a matter of time before they find us, unless we get offplanet. Your ship is the only one that's landed or departed from Gobindi in weeks. We need it."

"You're going to steal the ship!" she said. "You *are* pirates!"

"If we had wanted to steal it, we would have done that already," Wedge replied. "We just need a ride offplanet. You'll be doing the galaxy a favor—unless, that is, I'm wrong, and you really are part of the Empire."

"Well, I'm not!" Tash snapped. She was no longer nervous, but she still felt strangely warm, and her breath was short. "I hate the Empire. They killed my parents. They were on Alderaan when it was destroyed by the Death Star."

Wedge frowned. "You're from Alderaan?"

"Yes, and I'll bet I have more reason than you to hate the Empire."

Again the venom in her words surprised her. But she *did* hate the Empire. She had every reason to hate it. She felt hot tears form in her eyes. She didn't mean to speak these words—she was hardly aware that she had thought them—but they came out of her mouth. "I want revenge on them for what they did to my parents."

"I'm glad you're on *our* side," the other human joked.

But Wedge's eyes grew soft. "I'm glad we agree that the Empire's bad, Tash. But didn't you say you admired the Jedi Knights?"

She nodded.

Wedge considered. "My people, the people I work with, we believe in the Jedi, too. I've read a lot about them."

"Me too!" Tash exclaimed.

Wedge continued. "Let me tell you one of the things I learned about the Jedi. It has to do with that word *revenge*. Don't use it. Don't even think it." He looked hard at Tash. "The Jedi fought in many wars, but do you know what truly made them great?"

"What?" she asked breathlessly.

"They were warriors, but they weren't violent. They never forgot that their enemies were living beings, just like they were, with their own beliefs in right and wrong. They didn't get angry. They didn't hate their opponents. The Jedi always kept their minds on what they were fighting for, rather than what they were fighting against."

Tash listened to the words. They sounded like good advice. But they didn't sink in. Not hate the Empire? Not hate the people who had destroyed her family and her entire planet?

"I—I'm not sure I can do that," she admitted. If anything, she realized, her anger was growing by the minute. She could feel her heart pounding in her chest. The blood throbbed in her veins. Her bruised left arm ached.

Wedge shrugged. "I'm not sure I can either." He grinned. "But then, I'm just a starpilot. I'm happiest behind the controls of a snub fighter, not trying to use the Force."

Wedge paused again. "Tash, we have information we need to get offplanet. All transmissions are blocked. No ships can fly. Except this one. This ship's registry has unlimited landing clearance for this dock. We can fly out of here and no one will question us."

Tash recalled how easily the *Shroud* had docked on Gobindi, once they'd activated their telesponder code. *How did Hoole manage to do it?* she wondered. *Is he an Imperial after all?*

She never got the chance to answer. Behind Wedge, the other human cried out.

Something had grabbed him.

CHAPTER

11

Wedge and the Bothan jumped out of the way as the scar-faced human went down. Thick streams of slime had wrapped themselves around his legs.

A blob had crept aboard the ship.

The man cursed and tried to get up. He pounded a gloved fist into the blob. His hand sank partway into its gooey flesh, doing no damage. As he pulled it out, the glove stuck in the slime.

Recovering from shock, Wedge and the Bothan leaped into action. They, too, wore gloves. They used their hands to pry the blob loose from their comrade's legs.

Wedge and the Bothan pulled the blob away. It was heavy, but they managed to carry it to the hatchway and toss it outside.

"Are you all right?" Tash asked the scarred man.

"Fine, I think," he replied as his friends returned. He wiped his hand on his pant leg.

"I can't believe no one has tried to destroy those things," Tash said.

"The Empire won't destroy them," Wedge said quickly. "We think the Empire is *creating* them."

"What?"

The Bothan helped the scarred man to his feet. "The blobs appeared at the same time the blockade began. We think there's some connection."

"That Infirmary is more than just a hospital," Wedge explained. "We think it may be the home of the—"

"Imperial Biological Weapons Division," Tash finished for him.

All three Rebels looked as if someone had just stunned them with a hold-out blaster. Wedge looked at Tash. "Who told you that?"

"No one," Tash replied. "I found out for myself."

Getting over his surprise, Wedge continued. "What we can't figure out is *why* the Empire is creating them. The blobs are hard to kill, but they move slowly and they're no great threat. If the Empire is creating biological weapons, I'm not sure what danger these things pose."

Suddenly, without warning, the scarred Rebel collapsed. The blood drained from his face, and he lost consciousness.

They checked his hands and arms for injuries but found none. The blob hadn't bitten or wounded him in any way.

The two Rebels were confused, but to Tash, the man's appearance looked familiar.

"He looks sick," she said, then told Wedge and the Bothan about the virus Zak had.

Wedge's face grew pale. "That's it! That's what these blobs are for. These creatures must be carriers." He looked at his Bothan partner. "The Empire is creating a plague, and these creatures are delivering it."

"Do you think we've contracted it?" the Bothan asked.

"No," Wedge replied. "It must be passed by touch, or we'd all have fallen sick by now."

"Why would they be releasing it here, in the city?" Tash wondered aloud. Carefully she touched the lump under her sleeve. Could she have the virus?

But no, she hadn't touched one of the blob creatures. She hadn't been infected with anything.

"Test cases," Wedge said. "They're using the city to see how effective the blobs are, I'd guess. We're all lab rats." He nodded to his Bothan companion. "Come on, we've got to get back to the safe house."

Careful not to let their bare skin touch him, the two Rebels pulled their friend up and supported him with their arms.

Wedge looked back at Tash. "Please help us, Tash. We'll be watching. When your ship is ready to leave, we'll know."

Wedge and the Bothan carried their comrade out of the ship, first checking for danger. But the blob was gone.

A small hovercar was parked nearby. They slipped inside and skimmed quickly away.

The *Shroud* suddenly felt very empty. Hoole and Deevee were gone, and Zak was . . .

Tash almost dropped to the floor in panic when she realized.

Zak was still in the hands of the Imperial Biological Weapons Division.

CHAPTER

12

Tash slowly returned to the Infirmary. She wanted to hurry, but her legs would barely move, and she was sweating. Her discomfort only made her angrier. And she found that the angrier she got, the more energy she had. She could feel her heartbeat all the way down to her fingertips. The brown lump on her forearm thudded against her skin.

Staring at the Imperial Infirmary tower, Tash wished once more that she were a Jedi. She wanted to ignite her lightsaber and storm the Infirmary. She wanted to save Zak. But she also wanted revenge on the people who had hurt him.

"Well, why not?" she said out loud. Her voice, if she had stopped to listen to it, hardly sounded like her own. "After what the Empire's done to me, they deserve it!"

But Tash had never even held a blaster, let alone a lightsaber. As much as she wanted to fight her enemies, she would have to use stealth instead.

She rode the lift up to the tenth floor, where Zak was being treated. She hurried to the bacta tanks.

But the bacta tanks were empty. Tash thought quickly. *Deevee said he was going to check on Zak. So where are they?*

Tash saw the same medical technician who'd been attending Zak's bacta tank earlier. He was busily examining the bluish, liquid contents of a glass beaker.

"Excuse me," Tash said.

The technician glared at her, obviously unhappy to be interrupted. "What?"

"Do you know what happened to the boy who was being treated here?"

The technician looked at the bacta tank. "No, I don't." He turned back to his work.

"Was he scheduled to be released so soon?" she asked.

With undisguised disgust, the technician put down his beaker and called up information on his datapad. "No," he said tersely, reading Zak's chart. "He was supposed to receive treatment for another hour."

"Well, where could he have gone?" she asked irritably. She didn't like the way this technician was treating her.

The technician turned back to his examination. "I don't know. I suggest you wait for him in the waiting room near the turbolifts."

Tash stared at the technician's back for a moment, but

he did not turn around again. She could feel the blood pounding in her head. She felt angry. *Too* angry, she thought. Suddenly everything was aggravating her.

Tash tried to calm down and think clearly. Deevee had come to see Zak, and now Zak was gone. But Deevee followed Uncle Hoole's instructions. Had Hoole ordered the droid to do something with Zak? Or—Tash shuddered—do something *to* him?

Tash looked at the computer terminal she had used before. Everthing she needed to know was locked inside it. And Tash had the key: the name *Starscream*.

But before she could reach the terminal, the medical technician appeared behind her. "I thought I told you to go to the waiting room. This is an Imperial facility. We don't allow people to simply wander around."

Tash thought up a quick lie. "Um, I know. But I was supposed to meet with Dr. Kavafi, too. I thought he was at the bacta tanks." She could only hope that the technician recognized her from before.

The technician said, "There are tanks at the other end of the hall as well. You might try there."

"Thanks," Tash said, hurrying on.

She wiped a drop of perspiration from her forehead. Had something happened to the climate controls? The building seemed especially hot. Her eyes clouded over for a moment, and the hallway seemed to tilt dizzily. Tash panicked. Had she caught Zak's illness?

But the feeling quickly passed, and Tash hurried on.

She would worry about herself as soon as she had found Zak and discovered what her uncle was plotting.

At the other end of the hall Tash found the other set of bacta tanks, and to her relief, an unoccupied computer terminal. Someone had obviously just finished working at this station—it was cluttered with datadisks, an electroscope, and the leftovers of someone's lunch. Tash pushed them out of the way and was about to start typing.

"Still looking for Dr. Kavafi?" asked an accusing voice.

Tash whirled around. The technician had followed her. She was caught.

CHAPTER 13

At that moment, Zak and Deevee were making their way toward the landing bay.

"I still don't understand," Zak said to his droid companion. "I didn't mind getting out of the bacta tank early. Believe me, it was getting pretty boring in there. But why did we have to leave the Infirmary so soon? Why couldn't we wait for Tash?"

"I'm afraid I don't know," the droid responded. "I am simply following Master Hoole's orders, and those orders are to get you back to the *Shroud* as soon as possible. Tash should be waiting for us there."

But when they reached the landing bay, they found the ship empty. "I can't understand it," Deevee said. "I told her to wait."

"Yeah," Zak replied, poking his head into Tash's room. "It's not like her to— Yech!"

Zak felt his boot sink into something soft and squishy on the floor. Lifting his foot, he saw long, sticky strings of ooze stretch between the bottom of his boot and a thin streak of slime on the deck of the *Shroud*. "What is this stuff?"

Deevee recognized it instantly. "It appears to be the same material that those blobs were composed of. Tash and I encountered one when we first arrived." The droid quickly described for Zak the blob's attack and explained how he and Tash were rescued by the mysterious man named Wedge.

Zak's eyes lit up in alarm. "One of those things might have gotten Tash!"

"Zak—" the droid started to say. But Zak had already jumped out the hatchway and was searching the ground for more signs of the blob.

By the time the droid had caught up to him, Zak had reached the edge of the ziggurat that the landing bay was on.

"That thing left a slime trail," Zak said. "After it left the ship I think it crawled down the side of the ziggurat." He pointed down the steep slope of the pyramid, which vanished into the jungle steam far below.

"Unfortunately the side of this ziggurat is far too smooth for either of us to negotiate," Deevee commented. "I suggest we wait for Master Hoole to—"

"There's no time!" Zak insisted. "And there are stairs right over here. I think they go all the way to the bottom." Zak hurried for the stairs on the side of the ziggurat, without waiting.

"Tending human children," Deevee muttered to himself. "I would rather herd a shipload of Gamorrean slime cats."

He descended in pursuit of Zak.

He did not see the two shapes that came out from the shadow of a nearby ship and follow them down the stairs.

Tash found herself growing uncomfortable under the Infirmary technician's suspicious glare.

"I thought you said you were looking for Dr. Kavafi," the technician growled after a moment of silence.

Tash thought quickly. "I thought he'd be here," she said. "I was supposed to bring him this electroscope," she added, picking up the electronic visor.

The story sounded lame. She felt a drop of moisture trickle down her back.

The technician studied her a moment longer, and then said slowly, "Let's see if I can locate the doctor for you."

He put one hand on Tash's arm and used the other to call up some information on the computer terminal. "There you go," he said. "Dr. Kavafi is in a meeting on the twentieth floor. You can wait for him up there."

"Great," Tash said. "Thanks."

But this time the technician did not leave her. He escorted her back to the turbolifts and waited until one of the cars arrived. When it did, he watched Tash step aboard; then he leaned in and said, "Droid, take this young lady straight to the twentieth floor."

The door closed on his irritating smirk.

"Laser burn," Tash muttered as the turbolift shot up to the twentieth floor.

Maybe she could find a computer terminal there.

Still holding the electroscope, Tash stepped out onto the top floor of the Infirmary. The corridor was empty and quiet, lit by a few glowpanels and the light from a bank of viewports that looked out over the steamy floor of the planet. The hallway was lined with doors on either side, and the corridor curved away from her to the right and to the left, with no signs indicating where a computer terminal might be located. Tash guessed that this floor must be reserved for administrative offices. She had just decided to go left, when she heard a familiar voice approaching from that direction.

"I can't thank you enough for letting me in on your secret, Kavafi," she heard Uncle Hoole say. Tash had never heard her uncle sound so friendly or relaxed. "I'm sure it is a worthwhile endeavor."

"Think nothing of it, Hoole," Kavafi replied from around the corner. "There is no one I'd rather show my work to than you."

Tash scurried down the hallway to the right until she

was out of sight. She listened as Hoole and Kavafi reached the lifts.

"How do we get there?" Hoole was asking.

"Right this way," Kavafi said.

She heard them step onto the turbolift. Just before the doors closed, she heard Kavafi say, "Bottom floor."

Quick as lightspeed Tash dashed for the turbolifts. Reading the indicator lights, she saw which lift Kavafi and Hoole had taken. It was moving fast.

Tash jumped inside another turbolift.

"Bottom floor," she said.

A mechanical voice issued from a small speaker. "Access limited. Password required."

"What?" Tash couldn't believe it. *Access limited?*

"Incorrect. Correct password required," said the voice.

Tash thought quickly. *There must be a floor beneath the lobby—a secret floor. One that requires a password to enter.* "Password required," the mechanical voice repeated.

Tash braced herself. "Starscream."

The turbolift began to descend.

The lift moved at top speed, but the ride was very long. Tash felt the small chamber grow hotter, as if she was heading down toward the source of Gobindi's humid climate.

Finally the turbolift stopped. The doors opened, and Tash peered out. There was a long hallway outside, but it looked nothing like the Infirmary. The walls and floor were made of massive stones packed tightly together. Moss grew in thick patches on the walls. The air was heavy and so moist that puddles had formed on the floor.

She was inside the ziggurat.

Cautiously she crept forward. There didn't seem to be any guards or sentries.

Tash's heart was pounding. The hallway was dim, lit only by small glowpanels placed far apart. She wondered how far she was inside the ziggurat. She guessed that she must be close to the bottom.

Tash heard a soft, squishing sound echo faintly behind her. She quickly glanced over her shoulder.

No one was there.

She took a few more steps, and heard the *squish* again.

She looked back. The hallway was still empty.

Then, Tash looked up.

Over her head hung several oozing blobs, ready to drop.

CHAPTER 14

Tash turned to run back to the turbolift, but one of the blobs released its grip on the ceiling and dropped. She jumped away, and the blob splattered to the floor. It shuffled toward her, and Tash backed up a few steps down the hallway.

Tash knew she had to get to the lifts. She should never have come down here alone.

Maybe I can jump over it, she thought.

She never got the chance. A small *slurp* above her gave Tash just enough warning, and she scrambled out of the way as another blob dropped from the ceiling. And then another, and another. In moments the hallway floor was covered with blobs. Tash stifled a scream and ran down the hallway as the blobs oozed toward her.

She had no choice now. She turned and ran, knowing

that the blobs were too slow to catch her. After a few moments the creatures lost interest in her and began to wriggle their way back up the walls.

But they'd be waiting for her if she tried to go back to the lifts. She would have to face whatever else awaited inside the ziggurat.

The hallway did not branch off, so Tash knew Hoole and Kavafi must have come this way. She crept along, trying to keep to the shadows and watching the ceiling for any more of the slimeballs.

Tash's clothes were soaked with sweat. They stuck to her arms and legs like wet bandages. Her arm had begun to throb more violently. Peeling back her wet sleeve, Tash looked down at the lump that had grown on her arm. It was darker now, a dirty brown color that seemed to be spilling onto the rest of her arm.

It seemed like hours, but finally Tash saw a brighter light up ahead. The corridor became a wide plaza with many channels branching in different directions. Although the plaza was empty, Tash could hear muffled voices and the sound of machinery coming from the hallways.

Tash didn't feel safe, out in the open under the bright glowpanels of the plaza. The place could be crawling with stormtroopers, and she wasn't supposed to be there. But she had nowhere else to go. All she wanted to do now was get out of the ziggurat alive.

Keeping to the walls, Tash reached the nearest hallway and slipped quietly inside. Like the tunnel from the turbolift, it was dark, and she felt less exposed in the shadows.

Now if only the hallway led to an exit.

Up ahead, Tash could see that the stone walls of the tunnel had been replaced by a series of transparent plexiform panels. As she approached, Tash peeked cautiously around the edge of the nearest panel. Through it she could see a small bare room with white walls, floor, and ceiling. There was no furniture in the room, and no access panels for comlinks or vidcams. It looked like a cell. In the center of it lay one of the blobs. Checking to make sure no one was nearby, Tash stepped in front of the plexiform panel.

The blob sprang at her. It thudded against the transparent barrier and slowly slid down it toward the floor. It was huge.

The blob launched itself at Tash again.

Tash continued down the hall. She passed six or seven more of the transparent panels, each one looking into an identical room containing a blob.

Although the cells never changed, Tash noticed that the blobs *did*. They were growing smaller. It was as if the first cell contained a fully developed blob, while farther down the line they were still forming.

The largest blobs were the most violent, crashing against the plexiform that separated them from Tash. The smaller ones simply sat on the floor of the cells, quivering.

Passing even more rooms, Tash saw a blob that was just about the size and shape of a human man, lying on the floor. Tash could almost imagine a person underneath the ooze. The sight made her shudder.

The next sight made her scream.

The last room did not contain a blob. In it she saw a green-skinned Rodian—the same Rodian who had been arrested the other day. He was lying on the floor, panting for breath. A thick layer of slime covered his chest and his back. Strands of ooze crept down his legs and up his arms.

Tash felt her stomach turn in disgust. She saw the Rodian's mouth move. The plexiform was soundproof so she couldn't hear what he said, but she guessed by the snarl on his lips that he was swearing. He struggled violently against the ooze, trying to shake it off. Instead, the amount of ooze suddenly increased, almost burying him.

Tash's eyes went wide with fear. She had seen that kind of instant replication once before, when she had looked through the electroscope in the medi-chamber.

She knew she was looking at a virus.

The Rodian let out a scream and made one last effort to shake the disgusting mess off his body. But his struggle only made things worse. The virus replicated itself again, and the Rodian simply disappeared.

Tash tried to swallow, but her mouth was as dry as sand.

The blobs were people. People who had been infected with a virus.

CHAPTER 15

As Tash made this frightening discovery, Zak and Deevee continued to climb down the side of the ziggurat on which the landing bay sat. The stairs that had been carved into the giant pyramid reached from its highest level to its lowest depth. After 231 steps, they had sunk down into a gray-green haze of steam that rose up from the hot jungle floor. After 463 steps, Deevee stopped counting.

The steps were damp and covered with slime. The people of Mah Dala did not go down to the jungle, and no one had walked on the stairs for years. Moss, growing quickly in the humid air, covered most of the great stones that made up the structure.

At long last they reached the bottom. The jungle floor was soft and wet, and covered with a layer of rotting leaves and branches. Through the mist the trunks of enormous trees loomed like shadowy giants. The ground beneath them was covered with a layer of mud.

"I don't believe it," Zak said, pulling at his shirt collar. "It's even hotter down here."

"And far more unpredictable," Deevee added. "Dr. Kavafi said that the original Gobindi built the ziggurats so that they could avoid the jungle."

Zak looked up. The top of the ziggurat towered three hundred meters above them. "I can't believe the Gobindi just vanished," Zak commented. "You'd think a culture that could build that would be able to survive anything."

The droid wiped a thin layer of moisture from his photoreceptors. "Something obviously destroyed them. With our luck, we'll find that it was something in this jungle."

"That's why we should find Tash and leave as soon as possible," Zak replied.

Deevee pointed to the soft, squishy ground. The slime track that Zak had followed on the hard stones above was now lost in layers of rotting leaves. "And just how do you intend to find her, or the blobs?"

But Zak didn't look where Deevee had pointed. He was staring at a nearby tree. "I think they found us!"

The branches of the tree were alive with fat, wriggling shapes that had begun to slide down the branches. A dozen blobs had already reached the jungle floor and were oozing toward Zak and Deevee.

"Zak, I insist we turn back," Deevee commanded.

"No argument here," Zak replied. They both turned but found the stairs blocked. Blobs had crept up the sides of the ziggurat and covered the stairs. They were trapped.

"Go!" Zak shouted. "We can outrun them! We'll find another ziggurat and climb that one."

He and Deevee hurried from the spot just as the blobs closed in. Zak and Deevee were faster than the blobs, but the soggy jungle floor slowed them down.

Out of the corner of his eye, Zak could see more of the creatures dropping from the trees on either side of them.

"There's got to be another ziggurat around here somewhere!" Zak yelled, ducking beneath a low-hanging branch.

"There!" Deevee replied, pointing. His photoreceptors picked out a thick wall looming out of the haze. "It appears to be a large one."

Zak and Deevee reached the wall of the ziggurat ahead of the blobs. But they could hear the shrubs rustling, and the wet, smacking sound of the creatures wriggling along the tree branches and the ground.

"Judging from the design and size," Deevee noted, "I'd say we are at the base of the main ziggurat. The Infirmary must be somewhere above us."

"Great," Zak said. "So where are the stairs?" He could see nothing but a flat wall ten meters high.

"Perhaps around the other side," Deevee suggested.

They never got to find out. A horde of blobs oozed from the steamy shadows on every side. They were trapped.

Zak and Deevee turned to face the approaching line of slime. One of the blobs lunged forward.

But it stopped in midstretch and recoiled as a shrill sound filled the air. A bright streak of energy shot out of the gloom and struck the blob head-on. The blob scurried backward in surprise.

Someone had fired a blaster bolt.

On the blob's skin, a small black hole smoked for a moment, then oozed over and disappeared. The blob shuffled forward once more.

More energy beams followed, a barrage of blaster bolts that cut a pathway through the line of slime creatures. Through the hole stepped a human and a Bothan—Wedge and his Rebel ally. In moments they had fought their way to the ziggurat.

"You!" Deevee blurted as he saw Wedge. "But you are an outlaw!"

Wedge managed a grin. "I guess that depends on which side you're on."

He fired again and again, sending blaster bolts streaking toward the blobs. The energy weapons did not kill the creatures, but seemed to slow them down.

"How did you know we were here?" Zak asked.

"We saw you go down the stairs," the Bothan replied, never taking his eyes off the blobs. "We knew you'd need help."

"Thanks!" Zak shouted over the scream of blaster fire.

"Don't thank us," Wedge said. "Just get us off this planet! You can start by finding a way up this ziggurat."

"But there aren't any stairs!" Zak said.

Wedge poured blaster fire onto a bold blob that had charged toward them. "These ziggurats must have served *some* purpose. Look for a door!"

Deevee turned back to the wall. It was damp and overgrown with moss and fungus. The droid adjusted his photoreceptors to their sharpest focus and scanned the wall. He could see that deep grooves had been carved into it. Most of the grooves were covered with lichen and moss.

"I found something," he announced. With Zak's help, the droid peeled away layers of thick growth until the outline of a hatchway appeared. It was designed to blend into the stone wall, but they could see the thin seams that would let the door slide open. Zak located a small control panel and pushed several buttons, with no response.

"It's locked," he groaned.

Deevee's sensors had been drawn to a series of grooves carved over the hatchway. They were set in regular rows and marked through with curved lines.

"What is it?" Zak asked.

"It is written in the Gobindi language. But it is an extremely curious message."

"What does it say?"

Deevee pointed at the squiggly lines. "It is a chemistry

equation. It appears to be medical in nature. I think it is the antidote to some sort of infection.''

"That's not going to help us at the moment!'' Wedge snapped.

The blobs were creeping closer, ignoring the storm of energy Wedge and his companion shot at them.

"There's more here,'' Zak said. He peeled off more of the fungus that covered the wall.

Deevee's photoreceptors darkened. "Zak, if my interpreter program is working correctly, I'm afraid I know exactly what it says. And I know why this door is locked.''

"Why?''

Deevee paused. "It is a warning not to disturb this building. It marks the spot where a deadly virus was sealed up for eternity.''

CHAPTER

16

Inside the ziggurat Tash turned away as the Rodian finished his transformation into a blob. She had seen the Imperial stormtroopers arrest the Rodian, claiming he was a pirate. They had probably infected him with the virus on purpose, and then locked him in this cell inside the ziggurat. And the virus had slowly taken over his entire body.

A second thought made Tash shiver from head to toe as she remembered Wedge's warning. Was this the fate that awaited Zak? Had Dr. Kavafi infected Zak with the virus?

And what was Uncle Hoole's involvement? How could he allow Zak to be harmed?

Unanswered questions swarmed about in Tash's head like buzzing grass flies. But they were overshadowed by a sudden, uncontrollable anger. Tash had never felt violent rage before, but she guessed that it must be something like this. *The Empire had killed her parents. And now they had infected her brother with a virus!* She was sure of it. She wanted to tear the Infirmary apart with her bare hands.

The lump on her arm throbbed as her muscles clenched. At the end of this hallway there was a door. Tash pressed her ear against it, listening for any sound. Hearing nothing, she pressed the Open button. The hiss of the sliding door sounded loud in her ears, but there was no one in the room to hear it.

Tash stepped into a wide, round chamber. The room was covered in fungus from the floor all the way up to the ceiling high above. The stone floor beneath her feet was slippery with moisture, and the air reminded her of a sauna.

But worse than the heat was the fear that fell over Tash like a wall of durasteel. Something evil was in this room. Her skin crawled. She felt a million eyes staring at her.

Tash scanned the room, but saw nothing. Still, the feeling of being watched would not go away.

She considered going back . . . but to where? For all she knew, every other room in the ziggurat was crowded with Imperial scientists. No matter what she was feeling, she knew there were no Imperial soldiers in this room.

She stepped forward, and the door whispered shut behind her. Then, with a click, it locked tight. Tash threw herself at the door, but the durasteel portal was several centimeters thick, and there was no way she could force it open.

"This," boomed an ominous voice over a hidden loud-speaker, "is the final test of the Gobindi virus."

At the far end of the chamber another door slid open. Several stormtroopers shoved a human man into the chamber just before the door slid closed again. The man wore an Imperial medical uniform, but it was torn and caked with mud. His face looked drawn and thin, and his hair was dirty and matted against his head. Despite all this Tash recognized him instantly.

It was Dr. Kavafi.

"What . . . what happened to you?" Tash asked in bewilderment. Now Kavafi looked as if he'd been locked in a Hutt's dungeon for months.

"Wh-Who are you?" Kavafi asked in return.

Tash wrinkled her brow. "Tash Arranda. You know me. I'm Hoole's niece."

Kavafi pushed some strands of hair out of his eyes. "I knew a Shi'ido named Hoole years ago, but I've never met you before." He suddenly stiffened. "Never mind. It doesn't matter now. I'm afraid you have gotten yourself involved in something terrible." He looked around nervously.

"I know!" Tash said in sudden frustration. She was getting a headache, and her skin felt hot and itchy from the room's heat. "I thought *you* were behind the virus!"

"Not me!" the doctor said. He seemed more meek than before. "I came to this planet to do virus research. I did good work, too. But several weeks ago I was kidnapped

99

right out of the Infirmary by someone who looked exactly like me. An imposter!''

An imposter? Tash shook her head. ''No, it was you. My uncle Hoole brought us here so you could treat my brother Zak for a virus.''

The man shook his head. ''I'm telling you, for the last six weeks I have been locked in a cell at the bottom of this ziggurat. Someone assumed my identity and took over the Infirmary, replacing my entire staff with his own scientists!''

''Why?'' Tash asked.

The man pointed to the walls around them. ''I chose Gobindi for my virus research because the humid climate is ripe for breeding viruses. But as I began my research, I discovered that the Gobindi had done their own research before they vanished. They knew that the jungles below their city were festering with viruses, bacteria, and all manner of organisms. But the Gobindi's discoveries cost them their lives. They unearthed a virus on the planet's surface that was too deadly for words. Even the Gobindi, with all their knowledge, had no way to destroy it!''

''So that's how they disappeared,'' Tash whispered.

''They were wiped out!'' Kavafi said. ''In a last attempt to control the virus, the Gobindi identified all its original sources. Caves, stagnant lakes, and forest groves where the virus spread from plants to animals and back again, waiting for another host to come along and help spread the disease. Since they could not kill the virus, the Gobindi built huge tombs that—they hoped—would seal it away forever."

"These ziggurats," Tash whispered. "They were built to stop the virus from spreading?"

The man nodded. "When I realized this, I sent all the information to my superiors in the Empire, recommending that Gobindi be quarantined forever. The next thing I knew, a Star Destroyer arrived. I was thrown into a dungeon. Someone took control of all my experiments. But instead of stopping the research, they began to dig into the ziggurats, looking for the virus itself!" He shuddered. "I think they are using my virus research to create a galaxy-wide plague."

Tash looked at Kavafi's clothes, his ratty hair, and his bloodshot, swollen eyes. He certainly looked like he'd been in a dungeon for weeks. And his story was convincing. She asked, "But who would do something like that? Who could impersonate you so perfectly?"

Ten meters up the wall, a panel slid back to reveal an observation viewport. Someone was standing at the transparisteel window. "I could," the figure said.

It was Uncle Hoole.

CHAPTER

17

Tash blinked.

No, it wasn't Uncle Hoole. The face was too round and the body too squat. Plus, the figure grinned evilly. Hoole rarely even smiled. No, this wasn't Hoole.

But he was a Shi'ido, a member of Hoole's species. Which meant that he could change shape at will.

"That's how he impersonated you," Tash realized. "That's who I thought was Dr. Kavafi."

"A convincing act, I thought," the mysterious Shi'ido said, speaking through a comm unit. "It had to be, to trick Hoole. I even went to the trouble of actually healing your brother in a bacta tank, just to keep Hoole at ease."

"Where is Zak?" Tash yelled.

The mysterious Shi'ido grinned again. "At this moment I'd say he is lying on the floor of his cell, covered in the virus. In another few minutes, he should be just another—what did you call it, Tash?—a blob creature.''

Tash's knees felt weak. All this time she had suspected Hoole of doing something wrong. He was being fooled, just like she was. She could have talked to him at any time. Instead she had kept her worries to herself, and now they had all fallen into some sort of deadly trap.

''Do not feel bad, young lady,'' the Shi'ido said mockingly. ''You are dealing with an intellect far greater than yours.''

''Why are you doing this to us?'' Tash yelled.

The Shi'ido's face clouded in anger. ''Because you deserve it. And far worse. Thanks to your meddling uncle, you and your brother have ruined two of my experiments so far.''

''Your *experiments*?'' Tash could hardly believe what she was hearing.

The Shi'ido continued. ''I could have snuffed you out like an incense candle, but instead I watched and waited, giving you one last chance. And rather than give up your investigation, you headed straight here, to Gobindi.''

''We came here because my brother was sick!'' Tash argued. She was getting angry again, and the angrier she got, the hotter she felt. The skin around her bruised arm had started to itch. ''We don't even know who you are! It's a coincidence.''

''*Coincidence?*'' the Shi'ido roared. ''Was it coincidence that you showed up just in time to drive my living planet into a frenzy? Was it coincidence that you exposed Evazan just as he completed his resurrection serum? And was it coincidence that your very next stop was Gobindi, only three weeks after my virus experiments had begun?''

Tash opened her mouth to speak, then shut it. Who *was* this guy?

Dr. Kavafi spoke up and addressed the Shi'ido. ''Whoever you are, you are playing with forces beyond your control. The virus inside this ziggurat was not meant to be disturbed. If it spreads, it could create a plague of galactic proportions!''

The Shi'ido yawned. ''Actually, Dr. Kavafi, the virus you are so worried about was quite limited when I found it,'' he said through the comm unit. ''Oh, it was deadly enough. It took over its host at an alarming rate. But it wasn't very contagious. You cannot catch it by breathing the same air someone infected has breathed. It cannot live very long outside a hot environment. It dies quickly unless it finds a host.''

The Shi'ido shrugged. ''I've done some tinkering with the virus's structure. My new version is far more effective because it *can* travel through the air. At least, I think it can. We are going to test it. Now.''

In his observation booth the Shi'ido pulled a switch. Several vents in the walls and ceiling opened up, and Tash heard the whir of fans blowing air into the hot chamber.

The Shi'ido spoke again. ''You have already seen the results of the virus. It doesn't kill its host. It invades the body of the victim and wraps it in a cocoon of slime, then continues to feed off it. I'm not sure how long the victims live.''

Tash shook her head. She could not believe how evil this being was. ''The people who disappeared. The people who've been arrested. You've been testing the virus on them! How could you?''

The Shi'ido laughed. ''I'm going to do far worse than that. Once I'm sure the virus can infect people through the air, I'm going to test it on a much larger scale.'' He opened his arms wide. ''I have turned this entire ziggurat into one enormous air vent, with the Infirmary as the cover. Once the Infirmary is gone, I plan to blow billions upon billions of virus particles over the city of Mah Dala.''

''You can't!'' Kavafi yelled.

''Why else do you think I have arranged to trap these people on the planet for so long? There are so many different species here. It is the perfect test to see which species are affected by the virus and which are not.'' The Shi'ido paused. ''And that is the truly terrifying thing about a virus, don't you think?'' he said. ''You cannot see it. You cannot smell it, you cannot taste it. But it is there. It is there in the room with you right now.''

Tash and Kavafi looked around. The room looked no different than it had a moment before. But they knew it *was* different. It had been filled with a deadly plague.

''Actually you should be honored, Dr. Kavafi,'' the

Shi'ido said. "I've been saving you for this particular phase of my tests. And the Arranda girl, well, she's been doomed since the moment she arrived on Gobindi."

The Shi'ido examined some instruments in the control booth. "Excellent. It appears my virus dispersal unit is functioning according to plan. If you two will excuse me, I have to make plans to infect a city."

He closed his eyes, and his skin began to wrinkle and bubble. The next instant, the Shi'ido had been replaced by the perfect image of Dr. Kavafi. The false doctor reached for a lever. "You will have to pardon the blast shield I'm about to close. I can't let any of the virus escape just yet, can I?"

The blast shield slammed shut across the transparisteel viewport, and the Shi'ido was gone.

"What should we do?" Tash asked.

Kavafi shook his head. "There is nothing to do. We are trapped. You cannot avoid what you cannot see."

Tash suddenly remembered the electroscope. She had carried it with her from the Infirmary. "I *can* see them."

She checked the visor's controls and reduced the magnification so that she could see both the virus particles and the room around her. She put the visor on.

Her heart froze.

The electroscope revealed clouds of tiny, wriggling red creatures all around her. Magnified a thousand times, they were still little more than specks in the air. Streams of them gushed from the air vents.

"Over there!" she yelled to Kavafi, pointing to one corner of the room as she ran to the other. Using the visor, she could see where the virus clouds were falling, and where the vents did not reach.

Kavafi ran where she pointed. But he was right under a virus cloud that slowly sank toward his head. "To your right! To your right!" she yelled.

He stepped to the right, and the virus wafted to the ground beside him.

Tash could see the tiny creatures, like eels with bulbous, jagged heads, swimming through the air, trying to get to her or Kavafi.

Tash turned in one direction, and then another, but the virus clouds had fallen like a curtain over her. She had nowhere to go.

"What is happening?" Kavafi yelled.

"I'm trapped," Tash said. It was true. The virus was all around her. Sooner or later, one of the particles would touch her skin, and she would be infected. She could only wait in terror as the invisible death settled over her.

Tash remembered the Rodian turning into a blob in his cell, and shivered uncontrollably.

"Is there any way to fight this virus? Isn't there a cure?" she yelled.

Kavafi replied wearily, "No. All I can tell you is that it depends on body temperature and chemistry."

Tash watched the virus come closer. The urge to run was almost unbearable, but there was nowhere to go.

Kavafi went on. "Your body has a certain temperature, and usually it creates certain kinds of chemicals in your blood, your brain, and all the different parts of your body. But when your body changes—as when you are angry, or sad, or when you are sick—your body temperature changes, and your brain sends signals to produce different chemicals. Somehow this virus affects those signals and feeds off of them. But I don't know how."

The blood-red virus clouds were billowing closer. The doctor was still surrounded by a safe pocket of clean air, but the area around Tash was filling up with the virus by the second.

A moment later the last of the uninfected air vanished. The virus clouds descended upon Tash. She could see her skin crawling with millions of virus particles, searching for ways into her body. She gagged.

"What is it?" Kavafi called.

"The virus," she said. "It's all over me!"

Tash stared at the millions upon millions of tiny red viruses landing lightly on her arms. She could not feel them. But with her enhanced vision she could see that her arms had become blood-red.

But a strange thing happened. None of the virus particles wriggled under her skin. The virus was on her, but it wasn't getting inside.

It wasn't infecting her!

She described what she saw to Kavafi. "It is possible,"

he said. "Some species may be immune. But I thought all *humans* were affected."

Tash shrugged. She knew what she saw. She wasn't getting infected! Filled with sudden hope, she looked around the locked chamber. The blast shield made the control room unreachable. The ceiling vents were too high. But some of the wall vents looked low enough.

Tash plunged through a red wall of virus.

"What are you doing?" Kavafi yelled.

"Going for help!" Tash replied. She stretched and grabbed hold of the vent. Because it had been built into the old rock of the ziggurat, it came away easily in her hand.

She looked back at Kavafi. He was still safe in a little pocket of uninfected air. "Don't move," she said. "I'll be back as soon as I can."

Tash scrambled up the moss-covered stones and into the ventilator shaft.

It was like swimming through a sea of tiny sharks. The vents were still blowing the airborne virus, and wave after wave of the deadly creatures poured over her.

Not long after she'd begun her crawl, Tash heard a loud throbbing sound. She reached a point where the vent branched off in two directions. One branch was open, and virus clouds poured out of it.

The other branch was blocked by a small energy screen, probably, Tash thought, to keep the virus from spreading into other areas of the ziggurat. The field was strong enough to hold back electroscopic creatures, but not nearly powerful enough to stop her. She pushed her way into the energy field, ignoring the tingling she felt as she passed through it.

On the far side of the screen, the vent narrowed, and Tash had to squeeze her way through the tight space. The throbbing noise grew louder.

Reaching the end of the shaft, Tash wriggled toward a durasteel grate. It popped off easily, and Tash dropped down into a new chamber.

She was in the pump room. Like the other chamber, this one was round. Most of the space was occupied by an enormous mechanism made of gleaming durasteel. A pipe, twice as wide as Tash was tall, rose up from the machine, straight up through the thick stones of the ziggurat. This must be what the Shi'ido planned to use to pump the virus into the Gobindi atmosphere.

Still wearing the visor, Tash looked at her arms. The virus had stopped wriggling and had begun to drop off her skin. Both Dr. Kavafi and the evil Shi'ido had said the virus could only live a short time unless it found a host, and these seemed to have died.

Taking off the visor, Tash walked around the pump, looking for an exit. She spotted a plexiform cell similar to those she'd seen before, set into the wall of the chamber.

She recognized the figure inside.

"Uncle Hoole!"

The Shi'ido pounded on the thick plexiform and yelled, but Tash could not hear him. Hoole's skin started to wrinkle, and Tash assumed he would change into something large, like a Wookiee or a gundark, and break down the transparent barrier. Instead, Hoole suddenly became a rat-like Ranat. Then a tiny crystal snake. Then he transformed into a large Gank, and then again into Hoole. Pausing only to take a deep breath, Hoole began another series of changes—so rapid that Tash could hardly tell what he looked like as the transformations became a blur. What was he doing?

Then Tash saw the vent in his cell wall. She put on her visor.

A virus stream poured into Hoole's cell. The walls and floor were covered. Even Hoole's skin was covered—Tash could see millions of the little wriggling organisms working their way along his skin, trying to work their way into his flesh.

But the minute Hoole changed shape, the virus lost its hold.

As long as Hoole kept changing shape, he was safe from the virus.

"Surprising, isn't it?" said a malicious voice.

Tash knew it was the evil Shi'ido before she turned around. He was standing behind her wearing an oxygen mask. He pointed at Hoole. "Perpetual metamorphosis. He changes shape too quickly for the virus to establish itself. Ingenious, I have to admit. But I expect that from

111

Hoole." His voice was muffled by the oxygen mask. "You know, he proved difficult to infect from the start. I tried using an injection, and it didn't work at all."

He looked at Tash. "I should have known you would be resourceful enough to escape the hot chamber," he said.

Tash backed away from him. "That's not all. I also seem to be immune to your virus! It's not infecting me."

She expected the Shi'ido to look stunned. Instead he only sniffed. "Nonsense. The reason the virus particles are not infecting you now is that you have been infected since the day you arrived. I did it to you myself."

At that moment, Tash felt the lump on her arm expand. Greenish-brown ooze leaked through her sleeve and began to spread along her arm. Tash pulled back her sleeve and saw that the bump was the size of her palm.

She *was* infected. And the virus was growing.

CHAPTER

18

The Shi'ido smiled. "You see, you are not immune."

Tash felt her left arm grow heavy. She staggered and fell to her knees.

The false Dr. Kavafi had infected her with a shot in the arm that first day in the Infirmary. "You . . . said it was an antivirus to protect me," she said weakly.

"I lied." The Shi'ido stood over her. "I must say, you intrigue me," he admitted. "It has taken longer for the virus to begin replicating itself in you than in any other subject I experimented on."

He studied Tash as if she were a slab of meat. "I wonder why? You might be worth studying, but I suppose we will never know now."

When Tash looked at the quivering ooze on her arm,

she gagged. To keep from staring at it, she focused on the Shi'ido. "You're killing people."

"I have my reasons," the Shi'ido replied. "But then you already have an inkling, don't you? At least, you know its name."

Project Starscream. The code words that had gotten her into the ziggurat. The code words they had discovered on board the ship.

Project Starscream. Tash had no doubt that she was looking at its mastermind.

Tash felt her anger, long held inside, spew out. "You vicious—" she started to yell.

The virus was quickly growing, up her arm to her shoulder. She could feel slime slowly sliding down her back. The ooze wasn't *on* her skin—it was growing *out* of her skin. She fell to her knees and struggled to keep from fainting.

Tash could feel the virus starting to control her movements. She tried to stand up, but her muscles didn't respond. Something was fighting for control of her body.

The virus was taking over.

"Please . . . ," she said. "Help me."

"And ruin all my hard work?" the Shi'ido said mockingly.

Tash had never encountered anyone so absolutely evil.

The Shi'ido smiled. "No, I think I will leave you here instead. In a little while you will be just another mindless blob spreading my virus around the planet."

Tash tried to speak. Her jaw felt heavy. "Wh-Why?" She could barely get the word out.

The Shi'ido leered down at her. "Why? With this virus at my command, I will have a biological weapon capable of wiping out entire planets! Think of it, a virus that overwhelms its host, not killing it, but feeding off it, and spreading the virus again and again. Each victim becomes another virus bomb. This virus is a weapon that never runs out of ammunition."

Tash struggled to make her words clear. "Why . . . St-Star . . ."

"What is Project Starscream all about? Is that what you are asking?" the Shi'ido taunted. He laughed a muffled laugh behind his oxygen mask. "I don't think I will tell you. Now excuse me once again, this time permanently. The pump is about to vent the virus into the atmosphere, and I think I will have the best view from orbit."

The Shi'ido looked at Hoole one last time, grinning triumphantly before turning and leaving.

Tash's fear gave way to outrage. He had no right to do this! It was horrible beyond understanding. Tash heard the word echo in her head. *Hate.*

She hated the Shi'ido.

Hoole pounded on the plexiform. Tash looked up and saw her uncle point to the side of the cell. There was a small control panel set into the wall. She could free him!

If she could reach him.

Gritting her teeth, Tash struggled to her feet. Anger and

sheer stubbornness allowed her to stand. The weight of the virus blob on her shoulders made her feel as though she were carrying another person.

All she had to do was walk ten meters.

But her muscles seized up. The virus took hold of them, and she stumbled to her knees again.

Tash refused to give up. She felt driven by a powerful force: revenge. The Shi'ido had toyed with her and terrified her. He had injected her with a deadly virus and fooled her into thinking her uncle was a villain.

Tash staggered up the first step.

Revenge.

She took another step, and another.

Revenge. Revenge.

She would resist the virus. Her anger was stronger than the infection. She would win! She would have her revenge on the Empire and the mysterious Shi'ido.

In his cell Hoole pounded on the glass.

Tash was halfway to the control panel when the virus blossomed.

Thick tendrils of ooze burst from the center of the blob on her shoulder and wrapped themselves around her waist and legs, dragging Tash down to her knees.

The virus had grown stronger.

Tash stopped struggling. She couldn't defeat it. The angrier she got, the stronger the virus became. She couldn't fight against it.

She was only five meters from the control panel, but she knew she couldn't go any farther. She shuddered and blinked hot tears away. She was losing. Soon she would become another blob. She had lost.

At that moment Tash remembered what Dr. Kavafi said. Strong emotions changed the body, and the virus fed off of those changes. Strong emotions like anger.

And thinking of that, Tash remembered what Wedge had told her about the Jedi Knights: *They didn't get angry. They didn't hate their opponents. The Jedi always kept their minds more on what they were fighting for than what they were fighting against.*

Tash realized that she had been fighting against the virus, against the evil Shi'ido, against the Empire. She had been filled with anger and a desire for revenge. That wasn't the Jedi way.

Tash stopped struggling. She turned her mind away from the virus. She forgot about her hatred for the Empire. She forgot her desire for revenge on the Shi'ido.

Instead she thought about what she was fighting *for*. She thought about the home she'd had on Alderaan. She thought about Uncle Hoole, who had taken her in when she was orphaned, and about Deevee.

Tash felt her heart rate slow. Her breathing grew steady. She tried to remain calm. The anger drained out of her.

And the virus started to lose its grip.

Tash felt the slimy tentacles drop away from her legs.

She took a step forward, leaving a thin trail of melting ooze on the stone behind her. The weight on her back felt lighter.

Tash thought about her brother, Zak, who would stand by her through a meteor storm.

More ooze dripped away from her body. She stood up straight. She did not hurry. She stayed calm, the way she imagined a Jedi would be.

She thought about her parents. She thought about how much she had loved them. All the Imperial warships in the galaxy could not take that away from her.

She felt her muscles free up. The disgusting ooze still covered her arm and shoulders, but she was free to move.

She took one step toward the control panel, and then another. In another moment she was there. She pushed her hand wearily against the control panel, and the plexiform barrier slid back.

With unbelievable speed Hoole jumped out of the cell and closed the door again.

"Tash!" Hoole said. For the first time since she'd known him, Tash saw the stern Shi'ido's face break into . . . well, almost a smile.

Hoole located the controls and easily shut down the pump mechanism; then, with a shimmer of his gray skin, he transformed into a Wookiee. One swipe of his paw smashed the control panel, ruining the device. No virus clouds would fall on Mah Dala. Then he returned to Tash, shrinking back into his own form as he did.

"Uncle Hoole," Tash said weakly. "I thought you were working with the Empire. I thought you were behind this virus plot. I was stupid."

Hoole shook his head. "I allowed that Shi'ido to fool me. He was waiting for us. He allowed us to land on this planet in the first place. I walked into his trap, and I exposed you and Zak to danger."

"Am I . . . am I cured?" she asked. She could still feel the ooze sticking to her shoulders and see it on her arms.

"I'm not sure," her uncle confessed. "We will find out as soon as we get out of here."

"Dr. Kavafi," Tash said. "The real Dr. Kavafi. We have to get him."

"He is here?" Hoole started. "Where?"

Supported by Hoole, Tash brought her uncle down the passageway that led out of the pump room. The tunnel was deserted—the Shi'ido and whoever worked for him did not want to be on Gobindi when the plague virus flooded the atmosphere. After several twists and turns, Tash and Hoole found the virus chamber, where the battered Kavafi still waited. "Hoole!" Kavafi shouted when he saw them.

Taking the electroscope from Tash, Hoole confirmed that the virus clouds no longer floated in the room. The virus still did cover much of the walls and floor, but with Hoole as his guide, Kavafi was able to make his way to the door.

"Hoole! I can't believe—" the doctor began.

"We have no time for conversation, Doctor," Hoole said. "We must get out of this place."

They tried the tunnel that led to the turbolifts, but the path was blocked. Dozens of the virus blobs now filled the corridor—the evil Shi'ido's way of ensuring that no one came down through the lifts to discover his hidden chambers.

Hoole, wearing the electroscope, led the others on a twisting, turning route through the ziggurat's tunnels. They passed the virus chamber, and the pump room, and finally found a tunnel that led away from those chambers. Following this passageway, they came to a door, and Hoole quickly triggered the opening.

Tash found herself staring at the backs of Zak, Deevee, and the two Rebels.

CHAPTER

"Tash! What happened!" Zak cried, seeing the coating of slime that covered Tash's arm.

"There is no time to explain," Hoole said. "We must leave."

Wedge fired his blaster at the blobs again. The blaster bolt left a tiny burn mark on the blobs' flesh. "Good idea . . . but I don't think it's what these blobs have in mind."

Hoole looked up at the high wall above them. "Hold on," he said to Tash. To the others he said, "Please make room."

His skin crawled across his bones as Hoole changed shape. He had become a mammoth frog, a creature Tash had seen in the galactic encyclopedia. She clung to its bumpy skin. The mammoth frog braced itself, then sprang into the air, just catching hold of the top of the wall.

Quickly Hoole repeated the act until all seven of them were on the wall, just as the blobs converged on the spot where they had stood. Only when they were all safe did Hoole say, "Dr. Kavafi, we need a cure for Tash."

The doctor shook his head sadly. "I wish I could help. I do not know of one."

Zak and Deevee exchanged glances, recalling the writing carved into the stones over the ziggurat door. "We do!"

Hoole made the trip up the ziggurat in seconds flat, his body a blur as he transformed into a flying, batlike creature called a rawwk. A few moments later they heard the whine of engines as he returned, piloting the *Shroud*. The others scrambled aboard.

"What now?" Wedge asked. "Even if we do make it back to the top we'll have stormtroopers to deal with."

"I think not," Hoole replied. "The landing bays were nearly empty when I reached the ship. The Empire expected this city to be full of the plague virus. I suspect we will find that the Infirmary is deserted."

Hoole was right. He piloted the ship to the top of the ziggurat and landed in the shadow of the Infirmary. The gray tower had been abandoned. Hoole pointed to the Infirmary. "Doctor Kavafi, I'm sure you will find everything you need to make an antidote in there."

An hour later Tash lay in her bed, unconscious. Zak wiped perspiration from her forehead with a cloth.

"Are you sure she's all right?" he asked.

Dr. Kavafi nodded. "She is sweating out the last of the virus. This antidote is strong. It should return the victims to their normal state."

Wedge was anxious. "We shouldn't stay long. Eventually the Empire will send someone down to check on the progress of the virus."

"We'll leave shortly," Hoole replied. "But we may have an Imperial blockade to deal with."

Wedge grinned. "I can help. I have some experience running blockades."

The pilot looked down at Tash. "So these ziggurats that we thought were buildings were actually just giant containers for viruses? It's a good thing the Gobindi were smart enough to leave the antidotes carved on the outside."

Tash stirred. Then with a gasp, she opened her eyes and saw six concerned faces staring down at her.

"Am I . . . is it gone?" she asked.

"It seems to be," Dr. Kavafi said. "How do you feel?"

Tash took a deep breath. She shuddered, remembering the feeling of the virus crawling over her. "I need a vacation."

Everyone chuckled. Except Hoole, whose face was set in deep contemplation.

"Master Hoole, is something bothering you?" Deevee inquired.

Hoole nodded. "Indeed. I was just thinking—the Gobindi civilization vanished. If they could contain this virus, terrible as it is, imagine the power of the virus that eventually destroyed them."

Deevee's circuits shivered at the thought. "Let's just hope, wherever it is, it remains hidden forever."

EPILOGUE

Several days later and ten thousand light-years away, on a shuttle rocketing toward his own secret citadel, the evil Shi'ido scowled. His plan had failed. Hoole had discovered a cure, making his virus useless.

He would just have to start again with a new organism.

The Shi'ido put his hand on a small vial that was tightly sealed to prevent the escape of its deadly, electroscopic contents . . .

Hoole, Tash, and Zak continue their journeys to the darkest reaches of the galaxy in *The Nightmare Machine,* the next book in the Star Wars: Galaxy of Fear series. For a sneak preview of this book, turn the page!

AN EXCERPT FROM

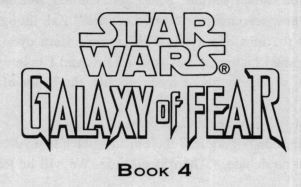

STAR WARS® GALAXY of FEAR

BOOK 4

THE NIGHTMARE MACHINE

The two Arrandas turned to face their uncle. Zak looked up into Hoole's dark eyes and his long, grim face. Hoole looked human—only a telltale shade of gray in his skin and his extra-long, delicate hands reminded Zak that his uncle was a member of the Shi'ido species. Of course, Hoole could *look* like anyone or anything he pleased. Zak had seen his uncle transform into creatures as large as a Wookiee and as small as a white rock mouse. Like all members of the Shi'ido species, Hoole was a shape-shifter.

And like other Shi'ido, Hoole usually looked either serious or seriously irritated. Now Zak expected that irritation to explode into anger.

To his surprise, Hoole merely removed the datadisk from the computer and said, "I guessed that your curiosity would lead you to the computer files as soon as I had given you some free time. And I have learned over the past month how resourceful you two can be." Zak thought he spotted the hint of a twinkle in Hoole's stern eye. "But my personal history is not your affair. And I believe that the less you know about recent events, the better off you are."

"But—" Zak began to protest.

"Please do not argue," the Shi'ido stated in a voice that allowed no debate. "There is no time. We will be leaving shortly."

With a swirl of his dark blue robe, Hoole turned and strode from the computer library, with Zak and Tash following. "But we just got here," Zak said. "Where are you taking us now?"

"*I* shall take you nowhere," their uncle responded. "I have business where you cannot follow. I have given Deevee instructions to take the two of you on a vacation."

Zak and Tash could hardly believe their ears. "A vacation!" Zak exclaimed. "How can we think about relaxing now? We don't even know what Project Starscream is all about—"

"Zak. Tash." Hoole stopped. His Shi'ido features suddenly softened with concern. He looked back and forth between his niece and nephew.

"You both must understand that this is not a game. I made a grave mistake when this all began. I should have removed you to safety the moment events turned threatening. My inexperience as a guardian has exposed you to terrible danger, danger that even I do not yet fully understand. The being who created Project Starscream is evil and unpredictable. And I am sure that he and I will meet again.''

Tash and Zak looked at one another. On their last adventure, they had come face-to-face with the scientist behind Project Starscream. He was a Shi'ido, just like Hoole. ''Uncle Hoole,'' Tash asked, ''who was that scientist?''

Hoole frowned. ''His name,'' the Shi'ido said, ''is Borborygmus Gog. He is extremely powerful and *extremely* dangerous. Now let's get going.''

''But how do you know him?'' Zak asked. ''What are you going to do?''

Hoole's face was as still as a durasteel mask. ''There are serious questions to be answered. I must continue my research. Now we must hurry.'' He started down the hall again as he continued to speak. ''I want you to go somewhere safe, where you will blend in with a crowd of humans and other species your own age. I do not want you to tell anyone where you are going, and once you are there, I do not want you to tell anyone your business.''

''Where are we going?'' Zak asked as he hurried after his uncle.

Hoole did not bother to turn as he replied, ''To Hologram Fun World.''

Hours later, on board their ship, the *Shroud,* Zak and

the droid DV-9 stood at one of the ship's viewports and watched the transparent dome of Hologram Fun World grow larger as they approached. Fun World was not located on a planet—it had been built inside a transparent dome, suspended in the vacuum of space. Zak estimated that Fun World was about forty kilometers long, the size of a small city. As the *Shroud* drew closer, he made out buildings, mountains—even what looked like an ocean!

"Have you been here before, Deevee?" Zak asked.

Making use of all his humanlike qualities, the silver droid managed to look depressed. "Certainly not," he droned. "As you are well aware, I was a high-level research droid before Master Hoole adopted you and Tash. Visiting an amusement park was not part of my programming." The droid aimed his photoreceptors at the approaching space dome. "Still, Hologram Fun World is a technological wonder. They say the holographic images look, sound, feel, and even smell like the real objects they imitate."

"Prime," Zak said. "I'll get Tash."

Zak knew just where to find his sister. She could generally be found in her room, reading datastories about the now-extinct Jedi Knights. She believed in the Force and in the powers the Jedi Knights were said to have; she even dreamed of becoming a Jedi herself someday. Until recently Zak had teased Tash about her dream, but during their travels with Hoole, Tash had gotten some strange, unexplainable feelings of dread. She seemed to sense when danger was near; just like (Zak had to admit) the legendary Jedi Knights supposedly could.

But when he reached Tash's cabin, she wasn't reading. She was sitting at her computer terminal.

"We're about to land," Zak said, flopping down on her bed.

The minute he saw the computer screen, Zak knew what Tash had been up to. She had been on the HoloNet, the galaxywide computer network. It was here that Tash had first learned about the Jedi Knights from a mysterious contact, code-named Forceflow. Tash suspected that Forceflow worked for the Rebels, who fought against the Empire. Forceflow had warned her about their last trip, to the planet Gobindi. They should have paid more attention.

"I finally got through to Forceflow," Tash said. "I asked him about Project Starscream and about Hoole."

"Did he know anything?" Zak asked.

Tash pointed to the screen. "Not much. He says that Project Starscream is a top-secret operation run by someone in the Empire. But he says it's not just military. It's scientific."

"We already knew that," Zak replied. "What about Uncle Hoole?"

"Forceflow sent me this." Tash touched a button on her computer and the information on the screen changed. Zak was looking at Hoole's file—the same file they had tried to break into at the Research Academy.

Zak scanned the readout eagerly, but the gleam in his eye faded quickly. According to the files, Hoole had been born on Sh'shuun, the homeworld of the Shi'ido species. He had been an excellent student on Sh'shuun, and eventually he had left his homeworld to study at the Galactic Research Academy, where he became a professor of anthropology. He had dedicated himself to recording the cultural habits of species across the galaxy.

"There's nothing here," he scoffed. "At least nothing we couldn't figure out on our own."

"Look closer," Tash prodded.

Zak scanned the file again and shrugged. He had read everything that appeared on the screen. Then he stopped.

He *hadn't* read what *wasn't* on the screen.

Four years of Hoole's life were missing.

Hoole had left his homeworld. Four years later, he enrolled at the Academy.

"What happened in between?" Zak asked.

Tash shook her head. "Even Forceflow doesn't know. But I'll bet that's why Hoole is so mysterious now."

Zak studied the screen again. "By the way, who *is* this Forceflow?" he wondered out loud. "How does he get so much information?"

"I don't know," his sister replied. "But I'm going to meet him someday. I told Forceflow we were going to Hologram Fun World and that I'd contact him again later."

Zak paused. "Didn't Uncle Hoole warn us not to tell anyone where we were?"

Tash shrugged. "But this is Forceflow. He's on our side."

Tash and Zak reached the cockpit of the *Shroud* just as the ship arrived at Hologram Fun World's docking station. They watched as Hoole guided the ship toward one of the docking latches. There, the *Shroud* would firmly connect to the transparent dome and its airlock, which would allow travelers to enter Fun World without being exposed to the cold, airless void of space.

Hoole deftly touched a thruster control. The *Shroud* nudged forward a few meters and came to rest squarely next to one of the entrance bays. As soon as the ship came to a stop, Hoole turned to his niece and nephew. "This is where we separate. Hologram Fun World is an exciting place—and I know you will be safe here."

"Where are you going?" Zak asked. "When will you be back?"

Hoole paused. "I should be back in a few days. As for where I am going, it is better that you do not know."

The Shi'ido escorted Zak and Tash to the hatchway of the *Shroud,* where Deevee waited, holding two travel cases in his mechanical hands.

Hoole opened the hatchway, which led to a sterile, durasteel airlock. Zak and Tash stepped into the lock and turned to look at their uncle. The stern Shi'ido's face had suddenly softened. He looked almost sad. He raised one hand in a brief goodbye. The outer airlock door closed, and a moment later Zak felt the floor beneath his foot tremble as the *Shroud* launched itself away.

"I hope he knows what he's doing," Zak muttered.

"I think he does," Tash said.

"Master Hoole is quite capable of taking care of himself," Deevee replied. "Now, come. You have an entire holographic world to explore."

Zak, Tash, and Deevee opened the inner door to the transparent space dome and entered Hologram Fun World.

It was like stepping into a dream. Before them, a pathway paved with green gemstones led through a gate shaped like an ancient castle. Beyond the gate, Tash and Zak could see the tops of dozens of buildings gleaming with the polish of modern technology. No two buildings were alike, and thanks to Deevee's many lessons in interplanetary cultures, Zak recognized the architectural styles of at least a hundred different species.

Forest-covered mountains rose up to the very top of the dome, which glimmered fifty kilometers above their heads. Air shuttles full of visitors zoomed this way and that, dodging herds of winged lizards and flocks of blue-winged gibbit birds. Music drifted toward them from different locations within Fun World. Zak heard laughter and shouts of excitement and surprise from the crowds of tourists. He felt as if the entire galaxy had been stuffed inside the transparent walls of the dome.

"Prime," he whispered under his breath.

"No kidding," Tash agreed.

"I suppose," Deevee said, "if one likes this sort of thing."

As they walked toward the old-fashioned stone gate, two young humans on mini-skyhoppers whizzed by overhead. One of them turned a loop in midair, waved at Zak and Tash, then flew away with a laugh.

Maybe this place will be fun after all, Zak thought as he stepped through the gate.

His thoughts were interrupted by a sudden angry roar that shook the entire dome from top to bottom. A blast of stinking breath washed up against Zak like a hot wind. He looked up . . . and up . . . and up.

Into the drooling, fanged mouth of a very hungry rancor.

ABOUT THE AUTHOR

John Whitman has written several interactive adventures for *Where in the World Is Carmen Sandiego?,* as well as many Star Wars stories for audio and print. He is an executive editor for Time Warner AudioBooks and lives in Los Angeles.